CW00867563

The Reality of
Saving Yourself

The Reality of Saving Yourself

Thomas Curry

Copyright © 2019 by Thomas Curry.

Library of Congress Control Number:		2019904223
ISBN:	Hardcover	978-1-7960-2677-1
	Softcover	978-1-7960-2676-4
	eBook	978-1-7960-2675-7

All rights reserved. No part of this book may be reproduced or transmitted in any form or by any means, electronic or mechanical, including photocopying, recording, or by any information storage and retrieval system, without permission in writing from the copyright owner.

This is a work of fiction. Names, characters, places and incidents either are the product of the author's imagination or are used fictitiously, and any resemblance to any actual persons, living or dead, events, or locales is entirely coincidental.

Any people depicted in stock imagery provided by Getty Images are models, and such images are being used for illustrative purposes only.
Certain stock imagery © Getty Images.

Print information available on the last page.

Rev. date: 04/10/2019

To order additional copies of this book, contact:
Xlibris
1-888-795-4274
www.Xlibris.com
Orders@Xlibris.com
793682

CONTENTS

Chapter 1

Bad Dreams

Ext.: Mall parking lot, afternoon
A van is parked and some voices come from it.

FIRST VOICE
Hey, here he comes, get ready.

SECOND VOICE
Yeah, let's do this, put this on.

Int.: Van, afternoon
The driver takes out two ski-masks. He gives one of them to his passenger. The two men put the mask on and open the side door and get out.

Ext.: Mall parking lot

A man and a little girl are leaving the mall. She's holding the man's hand as they walk through the turnstile to the parking lot. They are just a few rows from the car when the girl bends down to tie up her shoelace, and that's when he saw the two men walking toward them. He tightens the grip on her hand, and starts to walk briskly to his car. The two masked men match his pace, and start to gain on them. The man starts to run. He pulls the girl so fast she drops the ice-cream cone she's eating. They make it to the car in time to get away, but he's shaking so bad that he can't get the key into the lock. He sees their shadow in the door so he stops fumbling with the lock. He drops his hand with the key down beside, and let the keys slide out to the ground. His other hand is still holding the girl.

LITTLE GIRL

Daddy

The man turns around and puts the girl behind him. The tall guy is within three feet of them. He looks the guy in the eyes as though he can see past his ski-mask.

FRANKY (the man with the little girl)
What do you want? Take my wallet, take the car.
But hey, I'm with my little girl.

The tall man didn't say a word; he just stares at Franky. As Franky looks into his eyes, he can see that this is no robbery—it's personal.

TOSHA (little girl)
Daddy, I'm scared.

FRANKY
Hey, man, whatever this is, let my little girl go. Whatever this is about, she has nothing to do with it. She's just a little girl—let her go!

The two men are just looking at Franky, with their guns out.

TALL GUY
Shoot him, but shoot the little bitch first.

The other guy aims his gun at Tosha, and Franky drops and covers her up with his body. As the gun is going off—*Pop! Pop! Pop!*—he's trying to shield his daughter, but he can't protect her because the bullets are going straight through him and into her.

TOSHA
Daddy, it hurts! I want to go home!

The men stop shooting as Franky lie on the ground looking at Tosha's lifeless body.

FRANKY
Nooooo! Please, Lord, no!

He hears the loud sirens, but the closer they get, the softer the sound until it just turns into an alarm clock going off. Franky jumps up.

FRANKY
Tosha!

He's trembling and in a cold sweat, and then realizes it was all just a bad dream.

FRANKY
Thank you, God!

Franky is sitting on the side of his bed, shaking.

VO

Lately, I've been having some awful nightmares. I could live with the nightmares, but the thought of my past hurting my daughter's future, hell nawl, me, or my enemies couldn't live with that one. The nightmares started three months ago, the day I got custody of Tosha . . . my daughter.

The people in my family repeatedly tell me to get over it. They say it's in the past. Some even say, "Man the fuck up and let it go."

Lately, I find myself saying to Mrs. Toliver, "I'm sorry, boss lady, for being so sluggish but I'm having those dreams, and I can't get a wink of sleep." She would suggest I see a shrink, or talk to somebody, but not just any therapist. She recommended someone that helped her in the pass. My reply would always be, "Yeah, okay. Maybe," but at the back of my mind it would be, "Black men from the ghetto don't see shrinks."

The dreams got worse, and my anxiety got heightened to the point I thought about carrying a weapon . That left me no choice. I had to seek some help after entertaining the thought of getting a gun even if it was for protection. The first time I met my therapist, it was on a Monday afternoon, and I was the last client. I had been in the waiting room for about an hour, and then the receptionist said, "You can go on in. Dr. Cushner will be with you in a minute." I felt like a spy caught behind enemy lines, waiting for the enemy to try and make me tell all the secrets. I knew any second some mad doctor with a German accent will come in with a bald pin hammer, and some pliers to extract everything I knew. I guess it can feel like that at your first visit to a shrink.

I'm sitting patiently on the couch, waiting for some guy named Dr. Cushner to come in. The door opens, and in walks a woman, and not a bad-looking woman, if I may add. She was a tall, dark sister with silky black shoulder-length hair. She held out her hand and said, "Hello, my name is Dr. Cushner." For a second or two, I didn't say anything. I had lost my breath, and I was trying to catch it.

When she told me who she was, I gathered myself and said in my most masculine voice, "Hi, my name is Frank Smith, but everybody calls me Franky B."

I guess that was the male chauvinist in me because to my surprise, Dr. Cushner wasn't an old white guy. The doctor had tuned out to be a beautiful black woman. The woman had a look that made you feel comfortable about telling her certain things, so I did.

I started off by trying to tell her about the origin of my name. I kinda forgot what the B even stands for. One of my aunts said my uncle gave me the B; she said it was for *Bad*, but I don't know, maybe. If that is true, then it couldn't be a more fitting name for me. As the weeks, months, and a few years of our sessions went by, I managed to tell Dr. Cushner the harsh, but true story of my life.

Actually I had three lives: life before drugs, life when I was doing drugs, and life after drugs. Those first two lives I lived don't seem like it was me at all. Life before drugs seemed like there was no love. No one loved me, and I didn't love anyone, not even myself. Now, existing while I was on drugs had some love there, even if it was one-sided. I was in love with that dope pipe, but it didn't love me back. It snatched the very spark of humanity from my soul. When I look back on my child and young adulthood, it seems like it was just one big mistake after another. I guess everything happens for a reason. At least, that is what people have been telling me my whole life. If you ask me, my life was screwed up sixteen years even before I was born.

Chapter 2

Meeting the Family

My mother was sixteen years older than me, and she was born to a teenage mother also. Grandma moved from Mississippi to Chicago at the tender age of fifteen. She came to find a better way of life and to give birth to my mother. My grandmother had no money, education, or hope. She named my mother Ryan Hope Smith. Every time Grandma would say my mother's name, it would be in a strong North Ireland accent; but needless, to say we are not Irish. She named her after a soap opera.

She didn't know anyone personally that she wanted to name her baby after. She wanted her beautiful little baby girl to grow up, and do better than she did. Grandma knew she couldn't give her wealth or anything that would give her a head start on life. So she figured she would at least give her a famous name. You have to remember my grandmother was just a little southern kid alone in Chicago.

She didn't know any famous names, except the people she saw on TV. She didn't want to just pick a famous person from a book or something. After all, she didn't know what kind of person they really were—I mean what were they like at home behind closed doors. So when you think about it like that, naming your child after a famous and successful soap opera that you know everything about, not only is it *not* crazy, but it makes a lot of sense.

My grandmother always called my mother by her middle name, Hope. I guess deep down she was hoping her baby girl would break our family cycle of failure. Everyone in our family also called my mother Hope; they just didn't do it with the accent or for the same reason as Grandma. I think Grandma used the accent to imagine her baby was in a different life. I say this because she only sounded Irish when she was talking about my mother.

You can see why my grandmother called her Hope, and that is, because she was her hope. During that time my grandmother felt as though she had nothing to offer to life, and life didn't have anything to offer her. She put all her hopes and dreams into my mother.

Life is a little funny that way—you could look down the road and see light and hope, but in a blink of an eye there can be darkness and despair. Things didn't quite work out the way Grandma had planned for her little baby girl. At the tender age of fifteen, my mother got pregnant. Aw, déjà vu.

People in my family say that's what killed my grandma. They say she died of a broken heart. I never got a chance to see her because she died a day after I was born; I hadn't made it home from the hospital yet.

My mother brought me to a place of despair and resentment. They buried my grandma a week after I was born. My mother and my aunt Felisha started fighting at the funeral. The fight got so bad, the funeral director had to call the police. It started because Aunt Felisha was telling somebody that it was my mother and her damn baby's fault. I was only one week old, and already I was being accused of murder.

Two weeks after her sixteenth birthday, she had to drop out of school to be a mother to her fatherless child. She had no money, education, and you could see in her eyes that she had no hope. About my dad, from what my aunts tell me, he's a dark, skinny guy, with curly hair, and hazel eyes, the real handsome type. They say, I look a lot like him but minus the hazel eyes. Nobody on my mother's side liked him; after all, he was about five years older than her.

They claim they didn't like him because he was too old, and he was some kind of a thug. The real reason they hated him most of all is because he made me. Anyway, he vanished when she was five months pregnant. That was the last she heard from him. My dad had three sisters, an older sister La La, a baby sister Shay, and Twinky which was my mother's best friend. In high school, Twinky and Mama were inseparable. They did everything together; they even got pregnant at the same time. Her son Man Man is one day younger than me. I guess around the time Mama had to leave school, they started to grow apart. They say Mama got really bitter around that time. They say she was jealous and resented that she had to leave school, and Twinky was going to graduate, maybe some or all of that is true. But listening to my mama over the years, I know the truth. The day she didn't arrive at school and reported to the corner Arab store for work snatched her last glimmer of hope.

Chapter 3

The Changing of Things

My mama and I got along okay. I remember being happy as a little kid. I had a pretty, pretty life until my mother's twenty-first birthday. A couple of my aunts took her out to celebrate at some little neighborhood club. That's where she met him, this tall and fairly handsome guy. He said that his name was Billy Jones, but I don't know. He looked like the type to have an alias.

I remember when she first brought him to the house to meet me. They had already went out a few times before he was introduced to me. I was suspicious of him when I first laid eyes on him. He came to our door bearing gifts and wearing a big smile. He had flowers for my mother and a baseball and gloves for me, as though we were going to play. I knew that was a bad sign.

Somewhere, I heard a saying about "beware of the gift bearer." And boy, wasn't that saying true. It wasn't too long after we met before he moved in, and for a while it was okay. I had started to daydream about having a full family, with a mother and a father. I know that might have been a little stupid, but it was just a dream I had while I was awake. I did think he was pretty cool, even though he wasn't my real dad. He was the first man I had ever seen my mother with, and the first man to treat me like a son.

Once, he took me and my mother to a White Sox game, where he ran into this guy he knew, and he introduced me as his son. That was probably the cruelest thing he could do to me. To call me son made me want a father. I was using all the strength in me not to break down and call this man Dad, no matter how much I wanted to. I couldn't do that because I knew all the things he did for me was just to impress my mother.

Soon, everything changed. One night I couldn't sleep, so I got up to get some water. As I walked past my mother's room, I overheard him trying to get her to try some crack cocaine. She resisted at first by saying, "Baby, you know I don't mess around with that."

He was very persistent, you could say, relentless. After they went back and forth for a while, he eventually convinced her by saying, "Try just a little bit with me baby, and if you don't like it I won't try to give you anymore." I stood motionless at that door, waiting for her reply. Deep down in my heart I knew she was going to say yes, but I still was praying she would say no. Once she said the word okay, my heart shattered into tiny pieces. Life as I once knew it was now over.

Needless to say, she tried it; and like all the other hypes before and after her, that first blast was the best thing since Adam screwed Eve. I remember everything they said one to another, word for word. Like what they did when she took that first puff on that damn pipe. She choked herself, and how they both laughed. I remember standing outside her door wishing that she wouldn't be able to breathe.

They didn't even stay together that long; he was gone within six months. But that pipe he introduced her to, stayed with her until the day she died. I don't know whatever became of Billy, but wherever he is,

I hope he knows that I forgive him. I spent too many years hating that man and blaming him for all my problems and downfalls in my life.

Somewhere a long time ago, somebody said, misery loves company. As I continue to live I see more and more that is one of the most truest statements I have ever heard. That is why I can't hate Billy anymore because he was sick and miserable. He needed company in his misery. I just hope wherever he is, he has stopped sharing the pain.

When Billy came into our lives, my mother's heart was like a shiny glass door that opened one way. Not long after the time he left, it seemed as though her heart was dim and her bedroom was a fast-revolving door.

After he walked out, I had more stepdaddies than I can remember. Well, I guess I can remember a few of them, like Big Tony, who gave me this scar over my left eyebrow. He wanted some alone time with my mother, and I wouldn't go to sleep. So he got mad and slapped me with his high school football ring on his hand. Mike used to beat mama when he catches her high. Now the big problem with that was she was a crackhead and was high every day. Mama was a looker and she knew it. That was the end of them when Mike knocked out her front tooth.

And how could I ever forget good old Jeff. He was some crackhead thug that my mother and I shacked up with when I was six years old. One day, he and his friend came home and caught Mama with some guy. As the key turned and opened the door, I tried to warn my mother by saying out loud, "Hey, Jeff" but he ran up the stairs and burst into the door.

I heard Mama screamed out, "Oh my god." Then I heard a loud slapping sound and a big bang as though an elephant was stomping. His friend ran up the stairs and into the room. They both were beating my mother and the butt-naked guy. Somehow the guy was able to break free and ran down the stairs and out the door.

Jeff roared out, "So bitch, you like to fuck, well me too!" He called out again, "Franky, come in here."

I stood at the top of the stairs and in a soft voice I said, "Mama, mama, you okay?" She was about to call out to me then I heard a loud slap and my mother crying.

He holler out again, "Boy, get yo ass in here." I slowly walked into the room. He whispered something in her ear. Mama reacted loud and angry by saying, "Fuck you, y'all sum bitches, hell motherfucking naw."

Then he said, "Well somebody is sucking my dick."

I was standing in the doorway with fear and shock on my face. He walked over to me and grabbed me by the neck and said, "Now, who's gonna do it?"

His friend got this look on his face and said, "Hey, man . . . Be cool."

Jeff just looked at him for a minute, and then he said, "Shut the fuck up . . . Now."

Then Jeff look at my mother with his right hand around the back of my neck, and his left hand unbuckling his pants and said, "Now which one of y'all sucking my dick."

My mother told me to go to the other room, but he said, "Hell naw, bitch, you shouldn't have been fucking in the house with him here, so little man you gonna see all what yo mama do."

So I watched as my mother gave this man oral sex. I remember it like it was yesterday. That seen and his words still haunt my dreams with him saying, "And you better not let a drop hit the floor because if you do he is going to lick it up."

By the time I was seven, my mom had a hundred-dollar-a-day habit. With no money, education, or hope, she had to work the streets. She sold her beautiful body for this little piece of white death. Not only did she sell her body, but she sold her hopes and dreams. She was in no condition to take care of me. I was shipped around the family so much, from one relative to another. It had started affecting my school. I was missing so much school when DCFS stepped in and placed me in a home with foster parents.

That was when I first met Ms. Pack, my DCFS caseworker. It was also the first time I had ever seen a woman in a suit. There she was, this tall light-skinned sophisticated looking black lady, with sandy brown hair, hazel eyes, and a big pretty smile. She bent down where we would be eye to eye and said,

"Hello, Franky. My name is Ms. Pack," and then she reached out her hand to shake mine.

"Are you the lady I'm going to live with?"

"No, I'm your caseworker. I'm going to take you to meet some nice people that you will be staying with for a while."

I hated the idea of living with somebody I didn't know. When I told Ms. Pack about the way I felt, she said, it's just because it's new to me and to give it time. That wasn't it at all because I could have given it a hundred years, and I still wouldn't like it. That was because of one reason only, I knew my mother couldn't come with me.

When I was living with my relatives, I would see my mother from time to time. I might run into her over one of my cousin's house, or just in the neighborhood. Whenever I did see her she would always be high, but I didn't care because I loved her.

Once, my mother came over my aunt Felicia's house, where I had been living for a while. Aunt Felisha loved-hated Mama. Sometimes when she would talk about the good old times she had with my mother, she would laugh. She would laugh so loud that I would swear I could hear the love in her laughter. Then she would talk about my mother in the present day, and I would swear I could see the hatred in her eyes.

Mama knew not to let Aunt Felisha see her. She didn't ring the bell and walk through the door like normal people. She snuck in the basement where she knew I would be. She had this white guy with her. I knew they couldn't have known each other too long because he kept forgetting her name.

When I first saw her sneaking through the window, it was as though my dreams had come true. I had been praying that my mother would come for me. When she got in completely through the window, and I saw it was really her, I fell to my knees and said, "Thank you, Lord." Then I jumped up and ran to her, I grabbed her around her waist and squeezed her as tight as I could. She pulled me away from her body and said, "Boy, be quiet. Are you trying to wake your aunt Felicia up. You know that woman don't want me over here."

Then she went to the back door and quietly opened it. To my surprise and disappointment, a man walked in. I walked over to her and took her by the hand. I tried to get her to talk to me right away. I knew if she paid attention to me, and we were able to talk for a while, he would get mad and leave. It didn't work out that way. She took her hand from me and led me to the couch. She told me to sit down and watch TV.

Then she said, "Just wait here for a few minutes. I'll be right back, and then we can spend time together and talk."

My eyes started to fill with tears and I said, "Mama, please don't leave me!"

She shushed me again and said, "If you be a good boy, and listen out for Aunt Felisha, I will give you some money when I come back out."

The man came over by the couch where we were and said to Mama, "I thought you said this was your house, and you lost your key. It doesn't matter to me if it's your house or not. I do know one thing, I have very little time, so if we're going to do this, let's do it."

At that moment all I could do is think about Jeff. Was Mama going to do *that* to this man? Was this man going to beat her or me? I was so scared and confused I almost wet myself, but I decided to just scream for Aunt Felisha.

Right before I hollered out, Mama grabbed me and said, "Boy don't you fuck this up for me, now sit yo ass down and I'll be right back."

Mama took the man by the hand, and led him in the washroom and shut the door. About five minutes later they came out. She told me that she had to leave, but she would come back to get me soon. Then she gave me a dollar, a kiss, said she loves me, and walked out the door. I stood there staring at a close door with tears in my eyes. I didn't care that her breath smelled so bad, as though men have been using her for days. All I wanted was one more kiss from my mother.

During her visit, I noticed two things. The first one was she was getting very thin. That meant she wasn't getting enough to eat. The second thing I noticed, is that she was looking bad; she had a scarf on her head, and the clothes she had on, looked as though she had them on for some days. After that day, I always worried about Mama. Every day I wondered if my mother had something to eat.

When it would rain, I would pray that Mama would have a nice dry place to sleep. So no matter how many homes I go to, or how nice they were, I still waited for that day when Mama would come to get me.

Wanting to be with my mother has to be the reason I couldn't adjust to foster housing. I knew it wasn't because I miss where I came from. I was sleeping house to house on relatives' floors. Sometimes not even getting enough to eat or having no clean clothes to wear. It wasn't that my relatives mistreated me or anything, it was just that they had their own kids to take care of. That left very little means or time to take care of me.

Chapter 4

Game Is a Foot

Ms. Pack drove me to my new home; the drive was taking so long I fell asleep. Once we arrived, Ms. Pack shook me, and said, "Franky, wake up, we're here." I woke up to see this big beautiful house. It had grass and trees all around it. My first thought was "wow," but I didn't say it because of my second thought. My expression changed from amazement to despair as I thought about my mother. I wondered where she was or if she was safe. I wondered if she had enough food to eat or if she had a nice place to live. Ms. Pack could see something was wrong with me by the sad look on my face.

I remember her saying to me, "Don't worry, everything will be okay once you get settled in."

Mr. and Mrs. Pooly, my foster parents, had a nice clean house with plenty to eat. I even had my own bedroom, with lots of toys and real nice clothes to wear. They were pretty nice people themselves. I just never gave them a chance or let myself fit in. Every chance I got, I upset things, until they just couldn't take it anymore.

I remember the day I left the Poolys. I wasn't feeling good—I had an upset stomach and the runs. To try to relieve myself, I sat down to use the washroom. I was in agonizing pain as the waste from my body splattered and flowed out of me. Just before I flushed I dropped a few washrags in the toilet. Then I jammed the handle so the toilet would constantly flow. As the toilet ran over, I ran out of the washroom. I left the door open so the disgusting stuff coming from the toilet would run on to that nice new carpet Mrs. Pooly loves so much. About three or four minutes after I ran out of the washroom, I heard Mrs. Pooly say in this loud and angry voice "That's it! I can't take it anymore!"

Mr. Pooly held his hands on his head as to calm himself down, and then he said go in the room. I asked him what room. He said the room you've been sleeping in. I almost let out a smile because I had success. I knew by him not saying, "Go to *your* room," I was out of here and on my way back to Mama.

When Ms. Pack came to get me, I overheard them talking in the kitchen. Mrs. Pooly told her that I was a good boy, but I just had too many problems, and they didn't have the patience or time to deal with them. I jumped in the back seat of Ms. Pack's car with enthusiasm. I buckled up and said, "If we hurry we can make it to 71st street before dark."

"What, Franky?" said Ms. Pack.

I said, "Mama is always on 71st in the daytime."

Ms. Pack said, "Franky" in a kinda sad and subtle tone.

I cut her right off because I didn't want her to say she couldn't find Mama. I said in this fast and frantic tone, "I know she wouldn't be over Aunt Felisha's because they don't get along, but she's probably over one of my other cousins. If she's not there, she is definitely somewhere in my old neighborhood—"

Ms. Pack cut me off, by saying, "Franky, you are not going to see your mother right now. I'm taking you to stay with some nice folks for now, and I'm going to work on you seeing your mother . . . okay?"

My expression on my face changed, and my spirits dropped. I sat in that seat and didn't say another word.

Once I got to the next home, I was even worse. I felt kinda bad about that because they were pretty cool people. Besides, they had the same last name as me, and that made them even cooler.

It seemed as though I could not get kicked out of this house. No matter what I did, Mr. Smith would sit me down and talk to me. He would explain why I shouldn't do whatever it was I did. Every night before I go to sleep Mrs. Smith would tuck me in the bed, read me a bedtime story, give me a kiss on the forehead, and say, "Franky, you are loved." That made me feel warm inside like I was some kinda kid on TV. The warm feeling didn't last long as it quickly turned to deep sadness. For every kindness I received, I knew my mother received cruelty. I had to up my game, I didn't deserve to live this good. I had to think of something to do that was beyond talking to.

My last day with the Smiths, I woke up that morning to the smell of hot homemade biscuits. That wasn't the first time I woke up to an aroma of hot biscuits. I inhaled that heavenly smell once before. This was a couple of years before everything went haywire in my life. I was about four years old when I got my first smell of homemade biscuits.

Mama and I had just moved into our new apartment. We were so tired from lifting boxes all day that we didn't eat, and we went straight to sleep. That next morning, I woke up to a new smell; it was like hot buttery love in the air. I remember the biscuits smelled a lot better than they tasted. But boy did we have fun eating them. That day I declared hot homemade biscuits the official meal of me and my mother.

I sat on the side of this great big comfortable bed, and decided it was time for me to move again. I came downstairs and nobody was in the house. Mr. Smith had already left for work and Mrs. Smith was out back in the garden.

She hollered to me from the back. "Franky, the biscuits are in the oven, and there's some fresh orange juice in the fridge."

I hollered back. "Okay, I'll get it."

I actually went into the kitchen to get something to eat, but once I got in there, I knew this was my chance. I blew out the pilots on the stove and oven, then I turned the gas on its highest point. I went outside to the garden where Mrs. Smith was. I talked to her for about five minutes, then I told her I would be right back.

What I did next made me wonder if I was crazy. I went to the kitchen door and lit a match, I opened the door and threw the match in. The explosion blew me several feet in the backyard. About two hours after the firemen left, Ms. Pack was out in the front to take me to the next home. I kept on doing things like that, and they kept finding me new homes. I guess deep down somewhere in my mind, I thought if I kept getting kicked out of these foster homes, I would make it back to my mother. She wouldn't be on drugs, and we would be a happy family again.

DCFS is a joke, or maybe the joke was on me. The way the system works is they give you a pretty good home at first. The more homes you go to, the worse they get. In that case, I had made it to the big time. Big Time is what they call the homes with a couple of blemishes on their records. These homes are ran by people that have not quite met all the mandatory requirements for being a foster parent. But they slipped through the cracks because of the great need for foster parents.

When I first made it to the Hobbs' house I was nine years old. I realized that there was something very different and wrong about that place. For the first time in my life, I was scared. Ms. Packs told me on the way over there that there were four other foster kids there, so I should get along fine. Before I even saw the Hobbs' house, there I got a bad feeling about my new home.

Once we arrived and pulled up in the driveway, I felt a little better because the house wasn't nothing like I had imagined. We walked up to the door to be greeted by this middle-aged, overweight woman. She reached out to shake my hand, and said, "Hello, my name is Mrs. Hobbs, what's yours?"

I jumped back as though something scared me. It wasn't what she said, or even the tone of her voice. It was something in her eyes that made me afraid. I gathered myself, and tried to hide my fear. Then I shook her hand and said, "Hi, my name is Franky B." With a very firm hand shake, she said, "Please to meet you, Frank." As we walked in the house, the two ladies started to talk. I don't know what they talked about, but from the look on Ms. Pack's face, it wasn't nothing bad.

Mrs. Hobbs said to me, "Don't look so down, sugar. It's going to be alright. There are lots of other kids to keep you company." I couldn't figure out what it was that was giving me this strange feeling. Mrs. Hobbs seemed to be nice enough. She called all the other children into the front room so she could introduce them to me. She said, "This is Tony, he is fourteen, the oldest of our clan. This is Anne, she is nine also, just like you. This little guy is Andre, he is five. And last but not least we have little Jody. Yep, she's the baby of the bunch, she is twenty-one months."

Then Ms. Packs said, "Well, I will let you guys get more acquainted and settled in." She asked me to walk her to the door. When we got to the door, she kneeled down to fix my collar, then she said in a soft voice, "Take care, little guy." Once that door closed, I knew I went too far. All I could do is wish I was back at that house I just left. I watched her out the window by the door until she pulled off. I fought back a few tears before I went back in the front room where everybody else were. Mrs. Hobbs looked different, actually everybody looked different. When I entered the room I got a feeling that Andre and Anne were scared of something. All of a sudden, I found out in a big hurry what it was that changed everybody's expression.

Mrs. Hobbs looked at us and said, "What the hell do you little motherfuckers want now? The bitch is gone, so you can go back to your rooms." Everybody kinda scattered. I didn't know where to go or what to do, so I just stood there with a blank look on my face.

She screamed out, "Somebody, please take this little boy in the back with you all."

Then she said, "Lil boy, what did you say your name was? O yeah. *Fraaanky*. Okay, then Franky, around here when I say move, you move. So move your little ass in the back with the rest of them, okay?"

As I quickly walked in the back with the other kids, I thought to myself, "Oh shit!"

At first all the kids seemed to be okay. Tony met me at the doorway to show me around. Anne was in her room reading a book. He said Anne and Jody share a room. He also said I'll be bunking with Andre. He showed me where the two washrooms were and where the toys were kept.

Then he said, "My dude, if you want to, you can come chill in my room for a while. I have a cool racing set."

Everything seemed to be going okay, but I still had a bad feeling. My Spidy senses were going haywire. I told myself I was being silly, then I nodded my head and said to Tony, "Alright, that sounds fun."

"Cool, my dude, grab you a pillow off your bed because we're going to be on the floor."

I went in the room and I was getting a pillow. Tony stuck his head in the door and said, "My dude, it's getting late so you might as well hop in your pj's."

As I was changing into my pajamas, I noticed Andre sitting on his bed staring at the wall.

I said to him, "What's up, what you doing?" He didn't say nothing or stopped staring at the wall. I walked a little closer to him, he wasn't moving a muscle as if he was frozen.

I said, "Hey man, are you alright?" as I reached my hand to touch his shoulder. He quickly turned toward me with his finger in front of his lips making the sound *shhhh*. He looked over at the door to see if Tony was there, then he looked at me and shook his head no.

Tony sticks his head in the door, "You coming or not, my dude?"

Andre is back just staring at the wall, I kinda yawned and said, "Naw, man. I'm getting tired. I think I'm just going to lay it down."

The expression on Tony's face changed, as he quickly walked in the room up to Andre, pushed him in the head, and said, "I know, yo punk ass said something . . . but it's cool."

He looked at me and said, "Alright, my dude. I'll catch you later."

That night, I went to sleep with both eyes open.

The next morning was Saturday, and Andre woke me up so we could go in the from and watch the Scooby Doo Power hour. This boy loved Scooby Doo he had an old-looking Scooby Doo doll, but he held it as though it was his best friend. I asked to see it; he shook his head no and moved it to the other side of his body. I left it alone, and we continued to watch TV. Anne came in carrying baby Jody.

She said, "Hey."

I said hey back to her. Andre didn't say nothing; he just focused on the TV.

"You don't even have to tell me. It's the Scooby Power hour," said Anne.

I smiled, and said a little too loud, "Your name is Anne, right?"

She shhhhed me and said, "Please don't wake that fool up." Then she noticed the Scooby Doo doll and heard Tony coming out of his room. She handed me Jody and quickly turned the channel, then she sat over by Andre and snatched the doll out of his arms.

In comes Tony. "What the hell are y'all watching." She had turned to meet the press on accidently.

Then Tony said, "What the fuck is going on? Anne, what is that you're trying to hide?"

She replied, "Nothing."

He looked so angry as he said, "Bitch you got one minute to show me."

Anne brought the doll from her side.

He said, "Give me that shit. I thought I said I never want to see this stupid ass doll again." Anne reached out to give him the doll, Andre tried to grab it but Tony grabbed it first. He ripped it in half. Andre started to scream.

Anne held Andre close and muffled his mouth. Tony gave a chilling stare at both of them. Nobody said a word.

Tony waved his hand and said, "Y'all lame anyway," and then he walked out the room.

I said, "Don't cry, little guy. I'll get you another Scooby."

Anne told me that his real mother gave him that Scooby when he was a baby. She was about to tell me some more, but I was already up and on my way to confront Tony. As I was about to enter his room, he met me in the hall.

I said, "Hey, man. What the fuck is your problem?" I thought he was going to say something, but he just hit me in the stomach. As I was going down, he elbowed me in the head.

I lay on the floor in pain, he put his foot on my neck and said, "When I tell you to bring yo ass to my room. You bring yo ass to my room. Do you understand me, bitch." He put more weight on my neck until I said I understand. He removed his foot walked in his room and shut the door.

I knew right then and there that I was going to have to kill Tony. Anne came down the hall and helped me to my feet. She said it will be better for you if you just let it go, and just stay out of his way.

I thought that was great advice because that boy scared the shit out of me. The rest of the day went well, I hardly saw him, and when I did, he didn't say a word he just walked by as though nothing had happen.

Sunday night, I was getting my stuff ready for the first day at the new school. My stomach was a little messed up, so I put down the book bag and quickly stepped in to the washroom. I opened the door walked in and Tony was in there.

He looked at me and said, "What's up, my dude." He had the look in his eyes as though we were about to get real acquainted.

I said, "Aw, my bad. I didn't know you were in here." I turned around to leave.

He shut the door and said, "I need my dick sucked, my dude."

I looked him in the eye and said, "You might as well open that door because that shit ain't never going to happen."

Well, before I could finish saying *happen*, his fist was connecting to my jaw, the other fist to my stomach. I hit the floor in pain, then he pulled out some duct tape out of nowhere. I started to scream but he slapped a piece of tape across my mouth so fast. Then he wrestled my hands in front of me and taped them. As he was taping me up, he said, "If I can't get in one hole, I'll get in another."

Thank God, Mrs. Hobbs can't cook shit. He went on to pull down my pants, and my stomach couldn't hold it anymore. Soupy diarrhea shot out like a water cannon. It was like I aimed for his face. His eyes went red and he let out a yell, then he literally beat more shit out of me. I was bruised, bloody, and shitty but my virtue was intact.

Then he said, "If you tell Mrs. Hobbs anything about what happened tonight, I will hurt you. I won't beat you soft like I did tonight. It will be hard and really bad."

As he started to loosen his grip he said, "Even if you do tell her, she won't believe you anyway. Let's just say, she did believe you, she wouldn't do anything because she would have to make a report of what happened. DCFS may take you away, and that would upset her money. Do you really think she did not hear you trying to scream and all that noise we made?"

As he was talking to me, he was slowly removing the duct tape from me. I stayed calm and quiet until I was totally free.

As soon as he let me go, I ran screaming down the hall at the top of my lungs. I ran to Mrs. Hobbs' room, and I burst in, hollering, "He beat me, he beat me, and he tried to rape me." I abruptly shut up when I saw what was going on in there. As the door came open, her head looked up in surprise. I looked in, and I saw her and Anne in the bed naked. They were under the cover, but I could still tell they were naked. At that moment I knew she would not help me. I also knew in my heart I haven't seen the worst the Hobbs' house had to offer. The bruises he left was so bad that I couldn't register for school until four days later.

The next few weeks, I slept in the hall by myself. Tony didn't bother me anymore. He didn't say nothing to me; he didn't even look at me. That was cool with me because that boy scared me something awful. Like they say, all good things will eventually come to an end.

One night I was asleep in the hall, and all of a sudden something woke me up out of my sleep. It was Tony grabbing me by the face. He placed his hand over my mouth, so I could not scream out. This was bound to happen, and I knew it would, sooner or later. That is why every night when everyone would go to sleep, I would practice what I would do if he tried to hurt me. I taught myself to defend myself. I would practice kicks and punches half the night. My greatest weapon—I told myself over and over—is not to panic, no matter what happened.

Once I realized that this wasn't a dream, and was indeed happening to me. I put my self-defense plan into action. Somehow none of the kicks or punches I had practiced was working; he was just too strong. He pulled me into his room after he beat me to submission. He took out some duct tape and taped my hands and mouth up with it. At about that time, I forgot all about that great weapon I had, you know, the one about not panicking. Hell, I was one breath from having an asthma attack, and I don't have asthma. Once my hands were taped behind my back, I was beyond asthma attacks. I had passed out from fear. When I came to, I was taped in a chair facing the bed, as though he wanted me to see something.

He left the room for a couple of minutes. When he came back, he had Andre with him. I could see the fear in the little boy's eyes, but he didn't say a word. He just went over to the bed and started to undress, as though this was not the first time. He got totally naked, then he sat on the bed hold his head down and stared at the floor. Tony gave me this expressionless look, and then he had a big smile. I got a chill down my back, I didn't think I would make it out that room.

He walked over to that little boy and stood on the side, so I could see his private part in Andre's mouth. He grabbed him by the head with both hands and started to pump. I was desperately trying to scream out. I was nine years old, duct-taped, and seconds from going into cardiac arrest. And that was the second time I was forced to see something like that.

The anger is building up as I struggle with the tape and chair. The tears flowed from my eyes as Andre turned blue from lack of breath. He pulled out and Andre gasped for air. He didn't let the boy get three good breaths before he took him by the arm and turned him on his stomach. He gagged his mouth with a dirty sock. Then he mounted him, and started to have ravaging sex with that little boy. You could tell he was trying to hurt him. I sat there helpless, as I watched this act of terror. I stopped fighting the chair, I just sat there motionless with tears running down my face. It wasn't from fear for myself anymore. Mostly, it was because I had truly seen evil. The biggest part of those tears was for that little boy, who was being violently raped right before my eyes.

After he finished, he snatched the gag from Andre's mouth. Then he pulled up his pants, and walked over to me. I lost my breath as he reached in his pocket, and pulled out a box cutter. The only thing he cut with it, was the tape to free my hands. Tony left and went into the washroom. I snatched the tape away from my mouth and legs.

Once I heard the bathroom door shut, I got up and started running out the room. I stopped myself at the door, because I had to help that little boy. I turned around quickly, and walked back to the bed. I took him by the arm, and began to pull him up, but he yelled out, "It hurt so bad!" Then his voice changed, he talked as though he was out of breath. "Just leave me here, I'll be okay. He's not going to bother me anymore, he's finished for tonight."

I couldn't leave him there, the tears started to fall from my eyes again. I took a breath, dried my tears, and prepared myself to be as strong as I could be. I looked him straight in the face and said, "I know it hurts, but you have to get up. I promise, if you let me help you out of here, I will not let him hurt you ever again." I think he believed me, or at least he believed the look in my eyes. Even though it hurt him, he gritted his teeth, and let me help him up off the bed. As we were walking him down to Anne's room, Tony peeped his head out the washroom door and said, "Hey, Franky!" when I turned around whispered, "You're next." And then gave me that gruesome smile. I was not next because Mrs. Hobbs interfered after that incident.

Once we made it down to Anne's room, Andre couldn't hold his silence anymore. He started moaning so loud, that Mrs. Hobbs had to get up, and see what was going on. I could hear her footsteps as she stomped down to Anne's room. She hollered down the hall in an angry tone, "What in the hell is going on up here?" When she made it to Anne's room, she saw what all the commotion was. Anne and I were on the floor with Andre trying to console him. Mrs. Hobbs looked at me and said, "What have you done?"

I looked up at her with rage in my eyes, and contempt in my voice, "You know good and well I didn't do this."

She shouted out, "Where is he?" Then she marched out the of the room toward Tony's room, on the way stopping at the broom closet to get a broomstick.

She went into Tony's room. I heard the air being cut, and it comes to an abrupt slapping sound. Tony screams out, "I didn't do nothing!" The door slams. I could hear noises like furniture being moved around, along with the screams of a very disturbed twelve-year-old boy. She didn't beat Tony because of what he did to Andre. She beat him because of the consequences of what he did to Andre.

After she got through with Tony, she came back in Anne's room to see just how bad of shape Andre was in. He was messed up pretty bad. It took us half the night just to stop the bleeding. I told Mrs. Hobbs we should take him to the hospital, but that was out of the question. She knew that if she reported what had happened to Andre, they would investigate the whole house.

Anne told me that was the only time she had ever seen Mrs. Hobbs so scared. I knew her fear wasn't out of concern for Andre. By the way she was acting, I could tell she was not worried about losing the kids or their money. This woman was worried about one thing, and that was going to jail. Mrs. Hobbs knew if the authorities looked closely at the house, they would find out about what she was doing to Anne. She had to come up with a plan, to hide this heinous act of terror.

None of us went to school for three days because Andre was not healed enough to walk yet. Our cover story was, "The whole house came down with a touch of the flu." That story was only good for so long. On the third day, he wasn't ready to go back to school, but he had to go. Mrs. Hobbs knew if we missed more than three days, we would need a doctor's report for Andre to return to school.

Mrs. Hobbs drilled us hard for three days on that cover story. She made sure we knew what to say if anybody asked us why we had missed school. We went over every little detail, from how sick we were, to what kind of chicken noodle soup she gave us. She was relentless with Andre, it seemed like they were rehearsing for a Broadway play.

As cover stories go, Mrs. Hobbs thought she had come up with a pretty good one. And to say it didn't go the way Mrs. Hobbs had planned would be an understatement. About two hours after we made it to school, the assistant principal came to my room. She took me to the principal's office. When we walked up to the office, Ms. Jane, the assistant principal, told me to wait outside for a minute. I looked through the window, and I saw Tony and Anne, but I didn't see Andre. For some reason they didn't want me to see them.

When Ms. Jane called me to come to the office, the other kids were gone. They must have gone out the other door. The only people in the office were Ms. Jane, some DCFS people, and the police. There was another person in the office, and I was extremely happy to see her. It was Ms. Pack, and seeing her means I was ready to pack my bags and move on.

I told them the whole story, from the time I first arrived at the Hobbs' house to the present. I never saw Mrs. Hobbs again. I heard one of the police officers talking on the walkie-talkie, telling another officer to go ahead and arrest Mrs. Hobbs.

Can you guess how they found out about Andre? His teacher noticed a bloodstain on the seat of his pants. She took him to the nurse's office to have him checked out. Do you know what they found? Mrs. Hobbs knew that boy was hurt bad. She couldn't really stop the bleeding last night when he stumbled down the stairs. She just slowed it down, and hid it, or so she thought she did. She put a maxi pad on that little boy.

Her neglect of him was probably as bad as what Tony did—that's just my opinion. But I do know he will carry the scars of both of them the rest of his life. Andre was young then, so it was hard to know how this will affect him later. It seemed as though he was going to get the proper help he needed to get through this. There were no guarantees on anybody's future, so we only hoped for the best. Every night when I pray, there was always a word in for Andre. I asked God to look out for him and to make sure he doesn't share the pain.

Psychiatrists say 98 percent of all child molesters were victims of some kind of child abuse themselves. Also, 92 percent of child molesters were sexually abused as a child. To this day, psychiatrists are not all in agreement on what creates this copycat acts of rape, sodomy, and terror.

Chapter 5

Man Up

The Hobbs' house was the last foster home I ever lived in. It seemed to me, they had blamed me for what went down with Andre. Maybe not, but for sure I was being punished.

After that incident, I was assigned to another caseworker, and they put me in a group home for boys. All the boys in this home had been in trouble before, and was too hard to place. You had to be at least ten to get in a place like this. I wouldn't be ten for six more months, but somehow they made an exception.

They had taken the old YMCA building, and turned it into the Thomas Jefferson Group Home for Boys. It housed about three hundred and fifty boys, ranging from ages ten to seventeen. As you might have guessed, I was the youngest boy there. I remember the first time I laid eyes on the Jefferson.

Home.

Right after I left the principal's office, they immediately put me on a bus. I didn't even have to go back for my things because they were already packed and on the bus. I wasn't alone on the bus. There were about ten other boys along for the ride. I think they were all new to

Jefferson too. We were on the bus for about an hour when the bus driver said, "Everybody wake up, we're here."

As the bus pulled into the parking lot, a bob-wire gate closed behind it. I was scared because I knew this was a jail, just with a fancy name. Once we got off the bus, a big man in a police uniform said, "My name is Officer Taylor, and I want everybody to line up in a single file line."

We started to walk toward the entrance. Once we made it to the big double doors, Officer Taylor told us to stop and wait for a minute. As we were waiting for them to open the door, I noticed all the eyes were on us. It seemed like every window in the place had boys looking out at us. I lost my breath when one of the boys noticed me looking back at them, and threw a kiss at me. I said to myself right then and there, "Franky, take no shit from no one."

Walking through the halls going to orientation was a little scary. There were more eyes on us, and more sexual jesters. That wasn't the only thing that scared me. The building itself was scary. The whole place smelled like urine; the walls were two-tone, brown and beige. The floor I believe used to be beige, but it was now off black, and the lighting was so poor.

As we walked through the corridor, I could barely see because that place was downright dark. There was a bright light waiting for me on the other side of that corridor. Ms. Pack had come to make sure I was okay, even though she was not my caseworker anymore.

Ever since I had been in the system, whenever I would move, Ms. Pack would be there to see me in and wish me luck. This time was different. She was there because she was worried about me. When she saw me as I came through the corridor, she ran and hugged me. Her embrace was so tight that I could hardly breathe. I was happy to see her too. She pulled me back by both of my arms and squeezed me tight. I could see the seriousness in her eyes as she said, "Franky, this is no foster home. I know you're just a little guy, but you have to be strong in here. I want you promise me that you will let me know if anybody gives you any trouble. I'm going to try to get you out of this place. But until I do, I will be up here every week to check on you." She dried the tears from her eyes and said, "I have to go now. You stand tall, and remember Ms. Pack loves you, kid."

She kissed me, then wiped the last tear from her face, stood up, and walked away. About two hours after I got settled in, we went to eat dinner. Since everybody had dinner at the same time, it was a little crowded in the cafeteria. You have three hundred and fifty boys with only five monitors.

I was stopped in my tracks, as I watched some boys stomped one of the new boys that came on the bus with me. I was just standing there holding my tray, too shocked to move. This tall, light-skinned boy walked up to me and said, "Snap out of it, lil nigga. You in the hard knocks now." Then he said his name was JJ. When he shook my hand, he tried to do a gang handshake. I pulled my hand away, and said, "I ain't Folks."

He looked at me as though he was shocked and then he said, "Why not, what chyou a hook or something."

I guess he could tell by the expression that was on my face that I wasn't in a gang. He kinda looked me up and down, and started to laugh. I thought everything was okay because he was laughing, but then he said, "Awl nall, don't tell me you one of them pussy ass Newtrons."

He called another boy over to where we were. Once the other boy got over to us, JJ said, "Ant check this out, we got us another Newtron up in here."

Ant was a short, muscular brown-skinned dude with braids. He had a couple of scars on his face. He brought back memories of Tony when he said, "JJ, leave this punk alone, we'll catch up with him later."

A lot of these boys had been sexually abused, and in some cases tortured. The reason I'm telling you about their abuse and sexual history is for you to better understand why young boys would try to rape another boy.

The ones that were raped and abused weren't hard to find. It was like you could see it in their faces. They had this anger and hate displayed in their eyes. On my first night at Jefferson, some of them made themselves noticed.

We slept in dorms set up and nicknamed by your ages of the boys. I was in Dorm Pee Wee. There were thirty-five beds to a dorm. They were set up in rows of five. I was in bed 5-3. There I was all tucked away in my bunk, when someone slapped me in the face with a shoe. I woke up to see JJ and Ant with two other boys around my bed.

Ant said, "What's up shorty, you going to act right or what? It's time for you to be welcomed in properly."

I asked him what the hell was he talking about. JJ said, "You know shorty, what's up with some head, you got to suck our dicks."

I thought to myself, "What is it with these rapist ass motherfucker everywhere I go?" I started to tell him to get the fuck away from me, but I looked around and saw that it was a lot of them, and they were in a position to grab me.

Instead I said, "All of y'all."

JJ smiled and said, "Yeah, but if you do it right it won't take long." One of the other boys laughed.

I said, "Hold up, give me a minute." I sat up on the side of my bunk. Ant pushed JJ out the way and said, "I'm going first." He pulled down his pajama pants, and put his right hand on my head. I thought to myself, "I would rather die right here and now, before I do what they were asking me to do."

So I hit him in his dick just as hard as I could. I lay into him with everything I had, I got dick, nuts, and everything in the area.

I was able to hit him so hard because I was afraid, but not just that—I got mad. I thought about my mother and little Andre, and I found the big strength I needed in my little body. After I hit him, he went to the ground like a little girl.

JJ hit me with something on my hand so hard I thought it was broken. The other two boys started beating me too. As they were stomping me, I told myself to get up and not to panic. Once I struggled to my feet, I knew that I would survive this. For every two or three punches and kicks I received I threw one back as hard as I could. They were swinging wild and everywhere, but I was calculating and accurate just eyes, nose, and nuts. Still with all that, they were tearing my ass up. One of them got in a massive blow and knocked me off my feet, and this time I wasn't sure I could get back up.

I heard somebody saying, "That's enough, leave him alone." They stopped hitting and kicking me. I looked up to see this huge kid, holding his hand out and saying, "Come on, shorty, get up." He was about six feet tall, dark skin, with braids, and some tattoos on his arm. At first, I thought he was a guard, or counselor, because he was so big. He was a resident of our dorm, so he couldn't have been over thirteen. Jefferson was broke up into two floors, the young guys and the big boys. The young guys had the first floor with ages ten to thirteen.

That was how I met Big Bangs. It seemed as though we got to be friends the minute I took his hand. As he was helping me to my feet, I stole on one of those punks. Bangs didn't let him hit me back. He just smirked, as if to say, you're okay, kid. Then he took me to the nurse to get some stitches. Big Bangs wasn't just big, he was also the toughest person I've known in my entire life. That stands true to this very day. This kid would go up against grown men and win. Nobody messed with Big Bangs, and when I say nobody, I mean nobody. Since I was his friend, that meant nobody messed with me either. Speaking of that day, once I asked him, why did we become friends. He looked at me like I was crazy and said, "What in the hell, are you talking about."

"You know, why did you help me with those guys when I first got here."

At first he acted like he didn't want to talk about. Then he said, "You were pretty little, and besides you were outnumbered four to one."

I gave him this real serious look, and said, "You know what I'm talking about. Why didn't you let them rape me?"

"I don't know, Franky. It just wasn't right."

My eyes started to tear up a little bit as I said, "I'm not trying to trip, Bangs, but this place is starting get to me. People being raped, beaten, and abused in here all the time. I'm getting to the point where I can't tell if the screams I hear at night are real or in my nightmares."

"Franky, is this about the sounds we heard last night?"

I said in a mad and frustrated voice, "Yeah it is, and I'm a little upset because you stopped me from doing something about it."

He shook his head and said, "Little bro somebody told me this a long time ago. You fight the battles that you can win. Sometimes you have to fight those battles you can't win, but whatever you do make sure when the fighting is over, it's over. Last night was a situation, you wouldn't have been able to walk away from. That meant it wouldn't have never been over, at least not for me. There was one time, I took a chance stuck my nose in where it didn't belong. It was for somebody I felt was worthy of my friendship. I was right, you are worthy, and I'm proud to be called your friend and my brother. Since I've been at Jefferson I had never seen such a little son of a bitch put up such a big fight."

He said, I had reminded him of himself when he was about four. We both laughed.

Then he said, "The real reason is, when I first saw them punks step to you, I thought it was going to be another routine punking out. Man, did you blow my mind when you laid that first little fag out. After that, I wasn't going to let them hurt you. You didn't hit like no fag, so I didn't want to see you become one."

From that day, we've been like brothers, whipping ass and taking names. By the way, Big Bangs was just turning twelve when I met him.

That was almost two years ago. He was turning fourteen in a couple of days. The administration was making arrangements for Bangs to be moved to the big boys' dorm. The night before he left, he beat this guy an inch of his life. He did it with the Bible. He put a couple of Bibles in a pillow case and beat the stuff out of him.

Sometimes he would do stuff like that, just to make a point. After he beat him, he took out a shank and carved, "Thou shall not rape," on the boy's chest. Ironically, it was the same little rapist ass Ant, that started with me when I first got here. I knew he would probably do something like that before he left. He hated those guys. He just tolerated them, to get along in here.

Whenever I wanted to interfere in something, Bangs would give me the advice his mother gave him. He would say, "Pay attention, boy, because this is the only good advice that woman ever gave me. Don't shit were you live." I guess that's why he waited until he was going to move.

I wasn't worried about them getting me once he left. He took care of that. He always told me to make sure when you get that ass, you get it right. You know, when you whip somebody, make damn sure you whip them good. During the whipping, you inflict so much pain and fear in the person that they wouldn't dare to fight you ever again.

One of his terms for this was, "nip it in the bud." I remember fighting people and beating them down. I would get ready to get up off them, and he would pierce his eyes at me with this displeased look on his face, and say, "You need to get back over there, and nip it in the bud." I would know exactly what he meant. I would just start stomping whoever I was fighting until somebody stopped me or I killed them. In this place it's kill or be killed, but so far there's always been somebody there to break up my fights.

I was not worried about repercussions because Bangs was an expert in, "Nipping it in the bud." By the time Bangs moved, I had a reputation of being a bad ass myself. And if that wasn't good enough, Big Bangs was just in the next dorm in arms', fists', and feet's reach.

About three weeks after Bangs moved to the big boys' dorm, he went to jail for murder. He got into some kinda fight with two of those so-called big boys, and they ended up dead. There were a lot of rumors going around about what happened. People were saying Bangs killed them with his bare hands. Some people were saying he stabbed them with a knife. Others said he beat them with a frying pan, but everybody said he did kill them.

Everyone in Jefferson was talking about what had happened, from teachers to counselors, down to the boys—but nobody really knew. The big subject wasn't whether or not Bangs was guilty of killing the boys, only how and why he killed them. Now all of a sudden, everybody was an expert on Bangs's psyche. Even the janitors had an opinion on Bangs. Two days after the incident, I overheard two janitors talking, about something they knew nothing about. One of the janitors looked over at me and said to the other one, "Yeah man, that's his little brother, and he's crazy too."

The buzz around Jefferson was off the charts, that's all anybody could talk about. And the rumors just grew and grew. They had Big Bangs like some evil ninja killer. There was at least one boy that knew the truth, but ironically he was the one person that wasn't talking about it. I got really suspicious of Deangelo when he would go out of his way to avoid anybody that was talking about what happened with Bangs.

So I waited for the opportunity for us to talk in private, you know, man to man. When everybody was asleep I snuck over to his bunk and quickly grabbed him by the hair and put my shank to his eye. Then I said very calm and politely, "I would like to have a word with you."

Bangs always said, "Loud and out of control is not scary. It's just loud and out of control."

I guess Bangs knew what he was talking about because I saw the fear in that boy's eyes, and I heard it in his heartbeat. We went in the washroom and as I put my knife up, he started posturing to get ready to fight. I gave him the dark piercing Tony stare and then the smile. He knew right then that I was prepared to hurt him. He said, "Okay, man. What in the hell do you want?"

I asked him did he know anything about the boys that died. He seemed really nervous; he kept looking at the door and my shank. Man! Did he freak out or what. He started sweating and talking all fast about how he tried to stop Bangs. I started to suspect he had something to do with it.

I told him to calm down and tell me everything. I asked him, "So where were you during the fight?" He looked me in the face, took a deep breath and said, "Okay, if you really want to know, I saw Bangs and the two boys twice that day. Mrs. Rice, the fat old lady that work in the lunchroom, asked me to take some dishes to the storage closet. I had to pass the rec room. As I was pushing the dish cart through the stainless steel double door, I saw these two boy talking to Bangs at the doorway of the rec room.

"I thought nothing of it, so I went on to the storage closet. I guess it took me about fifteen to twenty minutes to put up the dishes. As I was walking back to the kitchen, I heard moaning in the rec room. I walked in as the fight was going on. The first thing I saw was one boy laid out on the floor with blood all around him. I looked closer and I noticed he didn't have a nose or an upper lip. I screamed out for Bangs to stop, but it was too late, Bangs was sitting on the boy and his face was gone."

I said, "Wait a minute, are you telling me that Bangs tore off a boy's face with his bare hands?"

"No, I'm saying I walked in as he opened his mouth as wide as he could and bit that boy in the face and ripped it as though he was a pit bull. When I screamed out at him, he turned around and looked up at me with human skin in his mouth and the devil in his eyes."

A guard was coming and interrupted our talk, but the talk was over—he couldn't tell me anything else. Deangelo lives on the first floor with us, but on this particular day, he was upstairs in the big boys' dorm.

After talking to him, I knew he had nothing to do with that fight. I knew right then as I saw in his eyes and heard in his voice. Besides from what I know about him, he couldn't have been involved. He just didn't have the stomach to fight anybody, besides he had asthma real bad. Deangelo got along in this place for over a year by keeping a joke in everyone's ear and a smile on their faces. Sometimes, he helped out in the kitchen for extra food privileges. On that day, he saw my friend and brother transformed into a monster.

The authorities decided to quietly send the two dead boys home to be buried, condemn Bangs to a life of imprisonment, and carry on as though nothing happened. On paperwork, it was stamped Solved, and under that, it said, "Gang related," closed.

The rumor was, Bang wasn't really a kid, that he was at least twenty-one. But the truth is he was only fifteen, but as big as any grown man. I put out my own official report around Jefferson.

"When you fuck with the bull, your ass get the horns."

THE REALITY OF SAVING YOURSELF

The police was partly right, it was gang related, but it went a lot deeper than that. The gang-related part of it was the two boys tried to get Bangs to flip Folks. The deeper part of it was, everybody knew Bangs was Blackstone to the heart.

He once told me that Blackstone was the only thing his daddy ever gave him. He never knew his father, but he was told he was a Blackstone. He told me, he truly thought his mother hated him. He would say with watery eyes how she would mistreat him when he was little. She would go into these rages, hitting him, and talking to him like she was confusing him with his father. She would show him scars that his father did, and ask him why did he hurt her. He told me she did that to him, and not his brothers and sister because he was the spitting image of his father.

Everyone in his family said he acted just like his father. They meant that in a negative way. He decided to live up to the hype and be just like his old man. So you can believe me when I tell you wasn't nobody going to turn Big Bangs from Blackstone to Folks.

Bangs and I often talked about how our family members seldom visit. We would fall out laughing saying if we went to the joint, we would probably see them all the time. To this day, I do not know why that was so funny; but it just was. We made a pact: "If one of us went to a real jail, the other would visit every chance he got."

I guess that was just a lot of talk and hopeful thinking. The day of the big fight was the last time I saw Big Bangs alive. He died mysteriously in jail. Having fatal accidents or becoming suicidal seems to only happen to the young, black, and poor. But this time it was no accident. Bangs had got in a fight with a guard. Before it was over, it took about ten guards to take him down. After the fight, Bang was laid out on the floor covered with blood. If you know Bangs, it wasn't all his blood. Six guards were injured in the fight, two of them were hurt pretty seriously. The one who started the fight with Bangs, they say, was hurt to the point he would never be able to work as a guard again.

When I turned sixteen, Bangs had been dead for a year. Six months ago, I got the news that my mother had died. When I found out, she had already been dead for two months. She died from an overdose of crack cocaine. They found her in an abandoned building. The lady that lived next door to the building called the police, after smelling a stench for several days.

One month and one day ago, I got in a fight with Tyrone, the general of the Gangster Disciples and two of his cronies. After the fight, I received ten stitches on my forehead and received one month in the hole. Tyrone will never see out of his right eye again; that tall kid I shattered his knee, so I am confident that he will walk with a limp for the rest of his days. And the other boy, he was the lucky one. I threw the first and hardest punch at him, and I had a short steal pipe in my hand. The instant my fist connected with his jaw, he was unconscious and out of the fight.

Chapter 6

Not so Fresh Air

Three days ago I was released from the hole. I had thirty long solitude days to come to this conclusion: "This is the last straw." I couldn't take Thomas Jefferson Home for Boys anymore, so I broke out and ran away. I didn't have to run, I could have just walked away. There was no one chasing after me to bring me back, and the thought of that even made me a little sad.

I had no money, no educated plan, and the more I walked around with my stomach rumbling, head throbbing, and feet hurting, the more I lost hope. As I was walking through neighborhood after neighborhood, I started to think of my mother. How she would walk these streets hungry, hurt, in rain, sleet, and snow. It made me dry my eyes and man the fuck up. I raised my head, shook my shoulders, and put some pep to my step as I was headed for familiar land.

The first day I left Jefferson was the beginning of my professional criminal career. Okay, maybe that's not entirely true. A person doesn't just wake up one day and become the kind of criminal I was. When I look back, I've been in training my entire life.

I was staying with my cousin Main and his mama in Motown. I'm not talking about Detroit. When you say Motown in Chicago, everyone knows what and where you're talking about. It's a ghetto neighborhood on the south side of Chicago, that was ran by the Blackstone street gang.

I guess, I'm doing pretty good saying I was sixteen, and I never really had a childhood, I never did well in school maybe it was because I had a few distractions in my young life. I really never got a chance to play on the monkey bars, go bike riding, or get a first kiss. In the life I lived, I couldn't have friends, except for Big Bangs. And a couple of guys in Juvi. Now Bangs wasn't really a friend, he was more like family. Hell, he was my big brother.

Things were about to change, like I said I didn't just wake up and turned pro. My well-known savagery at Jefferson had turned me into a ghetto superstar; and that meant money, cars, and yes, women . . . But still no first kiss.

Our crew had no leader, but Main was the one everybody looked to for answers. He was the real brains and drug dealer behind our operation. Whenever someone wanted us, they would contact Main. I even heard the phrase "Main and Them." So unspoken we all know that Main is the leader.

Twan was the one everybody liked; he was our mediator, and he kept hot heads cool. Now Twan is this talk mixed guy with wavy hair that all the girls like. I remember one time he and Main got into an argument. It wasn't nothing hell I don't even remember what it was about, but I can't forget this part.

Main said, "What the hell do you do here, anyway?"

When he said that, I thought how Twan kept us all calm. It was something about his reasoning that kept my rage at bay. If it wasn't for Twan, we would be at war with everybody. I'm not sure about the other guys, but Twan was kinda like my conscience. He didn't know this but he dampened my rage, and my taste for killing.

Lil Junior made us authentic and gave us our high position in the Blackstone. Lil Junior was the only one of us that wasn't brought into the Black P. Stone Nation—he was born into it. He was the oldest son of Junior Ross one of the founders of the Black P. Stone Nation. He was like royalty in this gang shit, so our crew had status from the word go.

For me, it wasn't a lot to say except, I was the youngest member of our crew. I was also the muscle, the terror, the fear in the night. Yes, I was sixteen and the fucking bogeyman in this neighborhood.

The Mo's started calling our clique VS. It stood for Vanish Squad I guess because we can make a motherfucker disappear. As our reputation was getting around, we did hits for money inside and outside the Nation, but make no mistake, we were Blackstone. Drugs were the biggest business for all street gangs in Chicago, and the Stones were no different. Yeah, we had a few little niggas on the street selling work for us too.

All Stones have to purchase their product from the Nation. So we didn't get the best deal; we paid what they said to pay. A lot of other chapters really didn't like it, and they made their voices loud and clear. If it got too loud, the Nation would hire us to quiet them down, and appoint a new general of their chapter.

Paying more for the Nation's products was okay with us because we had a little secret dope spot where we sell blows on the down low. Now the Stones had a treaty with the Cobras: they couldn't sell crack and we couldn't sell blows. Now what our crew was doing was grounds to break the treaty, but it was a small reason so peace went on. Both sides consider this illegal, but the streets being the streets and thugs being thugs, it wasn't severely enforced. Besides we were the muscle.

We still sold crack for the Nation, but it didn't pay shit. So Twan used his connections with his Mexican cousins on his father's side to get us a good deal on some blow. At first, we thought it was just going to be a few extra bucks. Yeah our little thing on the side turned into a big thing, and our main thing. It got so big we didn't make hits anymore. Throughout the history of man, whenever something gets something going good, there's jealousy . . .so we had to tear it down. People got to talking and word got back to Kelly and Dodge City. There was a group of project homes nicknamed "Dodge City" just southeast of Motown. The Cobras run those projects, and Kelly run the Cobras.

The treaty had been broken, but we didn't go to war, instead we went in business with Kelly using his cousin Big Don as a go between.

We didn't have too much trouble from the opposition or the controlling heads. So I guess since our crew was the muscle in Motown, and as long as our side thing didn't bother their crack business, the heads turned a deaf ear to the whispers.

We have another partner; he was not silent but he was discreet. He was one of my oldest living friends, and he was also one of Motown's greatest enemies. His name was Ronny, and he was the enforcer for No Love.

There was this one guy that always gave the Mo's problems, and now was becoming a very big problem for me and my partners. He didn't give a shit about how tough we think our street gangs were. Because he was a high-ranking member of the biggest gang in Chicago—the Chicago Police Department.

There was supposed to be some rules to this police-and-gangster shit, but this dude was breaking them all. Thugs do shit and the streets pay them; the police arrest thugs and the department pay them. And that was how it should be, but this white nigga and his band of corrupt cops were getting paid by both sides. Now we all have heard of dirty cops getting their cut, but this fool still busted us every chance he got. They called that taxation without representation, and that was a double no-no.

Now don't get it twisted, I'm not crying, and I know the game ain't fair. If nobody else was playing by the rules why should I? The streets got this stupid ass unwritten rule: You Do Not Kill Cops.

Sergeant Dorsey and his crew had been raping and pillaging Motown and the surrounding territories long before I got there.

All the heads, my cousin Main, even big bad Ronny and all the brothers that have any voice said, "That's how it is, he can't be touched."

All of them said the same thing when I asked them, why in the hell not.

"It will bring too much heat."

I said to them, "Fuck the heat."

The truth was, we looked death in the face every day since the day we said, "I am Blackstone" or Gangster or Cobra, etc. The next controlling factor has to be jail, but it shouldn't be. Jail was just an occupational hazard . . . so what are we scared of? The majority of the heads don't have balls so they would always vote me down, but in their heart and brains, they knew I was right.

The game had changed so much that I hardly knew what was what. I mean, you got Gangbangers snitching to the police on other Gangbangers just to eliminate the competition. You even got heads snitching on and killing their own people just for a few more inches of street. You got police killing young blacks and browns because they got skin in the street game.

A cop drove up to one of our young 'uns and told him Dorsey wants to see Main. At the meeting, he let Main know that he knew all about our side business, and that he knew that the heads knew. He also said we have not paid our taxes, and that we owed a great deal of back taxes. Now Sergeant Dorsey was no fool, he knew our strengths and weaknesses. He figured if he brings it to the heads of the Mo's and let them in on a few things that they don't know, like Kelly, the general of the Cobras in Dodge City, was one of our partners. He could also mention that Ronny, one of their biggest threats, was also one of our partners. What scared them about Ronny was if they had a coup across the Boulevard today, Ronny would definitely be the head of No Love, and maybe the head of the Gangster Nation. So you can see how we wouldn't want this getting back to the heads.

When Main told me we need to talk and to meet him at Lil Junior's house, I knew something wasn't right. Because we never met at Lil Junior's house or any of our houses. Besides, Lil Junior lived on the far west side. It was in a nice part of the city, but still in Vice Lord territory. Twan and I got there about the same time; the other guys haven't made it yet, and Lil Junior called and said he was right around the corner and he would be there in a minute.

This was just my second time ever coming to Lil Junior's house. Like I said, it was in a typical expensive bad neighborhood. There were two and three flat buildings, with everybody bunched up and no parking. There were some grass, a few trees, and it might be a little cleaner. On the way to his house just a few blocks away, I saw the little white and mixed punks throwing up the Vice Lord sign.

Now that I was on his block, I could see some niggas standing outside, so I said to Twan, "Lil Junior always trying to say this neighborhood is so great. Just look at them nigga down the street, I bet they down there slinging drugs."

Twan gave me this look and then say, "Yeah . . . and them Catholic school uniforms are probably their colors." Then he looked at me again, and we both fell out laughing.

THE REALITY OF SAVING YOURSELF   49

Since they weren't there yet, and evidently I had nothing to say about the neighborhood, I decided to talk about my car. Now with that I represented with my Blackstone mobile. Yeah, I had a tricked-out candy-red with two black racing stripes Chevy Caprice, and with the light-green tinted windows so you know I thought I was bad. When anybody saw my car, they just knew I was a Stone.

Just when I was finishing my speech on my car, the other guys were pulling up. And here comes Ronny in a black and candy-blue old school Lincoln with the Big Pay Back pumping out the windows. Twan looked at me with a smile on his face. I looked at him and said, "Not a word" then we both started laughing. Lil Junior opened the door and we went in.

Main got right to the point. "We have to start paying that motherfucka."

Lil Junior said, "Who you talking Mo?"

Main gave us the look, and kinda tilted his head, as to say, you know.

Twan said, "We already pay Dorsey."

Then Main said, "Yeah, but he knows about our thing, and he's threatening to break it up and start a war."

Ronny said, "Yeah we have to pay him, but I hate that pussy ass nigga."

Big Don said, "Dorsey's white."

Ronny replied, "What does that have to do with him being a nigga . . . Not a damn thing."

Main said, "I don't know but he seems to find out everything, but that's beside the point. He knows and we have to pay him."

Lil Junior says, "How much?"

Main said, "Twenty percent, plus back pay."

I straight out said, "Bullshit we need to nip his ass in the fucking bud! Hey, I'll do it . . . today."

Main said, "Mo, what are you talking about? Dorsey is not only CPD, he is sergeant of detectives."

I screamed out, "A dirty detective!"

Lil Junior said, "Slow down, Mo, with all that loud shit."

"My bad, Mo," I replied.

"Fuck it . . . we got to pay him," said Lil Junior.

"Now y'all know if this shit gets out in the open we not only gonna have to deal with Dorsey. It will be turmoil in all of our camps, and outright war with the heads," said Main.

As all this conversation was going on, I thought to myself, "This low life is as much fit to be a cop as I am." He is as crooked as they come. He tries to squeeze us for money and drugs. Every week, we have to give him a package, no matter what. He calls it paying our debt to society. Then he would laugh and say, "Hi, I'm society. Pleased to meet you."

My face was getting redder and redder as Main and the guys were talking about how we have to bow down to this bitch ass motherfucka.

My mind was everywhere but in that speech Main was giving. I did hear the last part of what he was saying, and it went like this:

"If this gets out in the open we going to have to fight for life. Now y'all know we will no longer be Mo's. And I personally don't want to go to war with the brothers over a few bucks. Ronny, are you ready to have civil war over in No Love, and what about you, Big Don?"

Then he said, "Hey, I'm not no head of nothing, each one of us get to vote."

"Fuck it, let's just pay him," Twan retorted.

Li Junior said, "Yeah, I vote—pay him."

From Ronny, "Yeah, pay him."

Main said, "Okay, we paying him."

Big Don looked at me, kind of shook his head, and said, "Man, we don't have a choice . . ." then he looked over at Main and said, "Pay him."

I had this disbelief look on my face, and before I could even say anything or vote, Main cut me off.

"It's been settled already, Franky. We're going to pay the man," Main said.

In my mind, if Main said it, I did it . . . until I didn't.

It seems like three months ago since we started paying Dorsey, we've been kind of at war with everybody. Throughout the city, there were chapters of Gangster disciples at war with their neighboring chapter of Blackstones. The Mo's and the Folks were two of the biggest street gangs in the city. Maybe the country. So with that being said, they were just naturally competing opposition. It was a little different with Motown and No Love . . . for a while we had peace.

No Love was run by Keith Avery aka Daddy Keith. Now the way I understood it, it was Daddy Keith and Mufaso, the head general in Motown, grew up together. Yeah, they were friends with a boulevard separating them. One was a Stone and the other was a Gangster.

I'm not saying that we lived in harmony with the folks in No Love because there were incidents here and there; but for the most part, we lived and let live. Peace was always good for the dope business.

I had something like a Daddy Keith and Mufaso thing with Ron Brown aka Ronny. Everybody knew that Ronny was Folks. He was also the muscle of No Love and one of the toughest thugs in the city. Some people even knew we were friends, but what they didn't know was how far we go back.

We first met in Juvi. On that particular day, there was some a commotion with the opposition. I was told to go to the neutral zone. When I got there, I saw Ronny Brown standing on the other side of the circle. Because of our unusual relationship with our neighbors across the boulevard, we try to settle things without death. Yeah, that means it's time to knuckle up. It was odd to see Ronny there, and even more odd for them to have sent me. When something happens and you see people like me and Ronny, it was way past knuckles.

Ronny had a twin brother name Donny. He was a civilian, and the first person to go to college in their entire family. So to say that Ronny was over protective of Donny was a fucking understatement. Well, that night, Donny and two of his friends were at a club and got into an altercation with some of the Mo's. There were punches thrown and some shots fired. There were five Stone's and they were getting the worst of the fight. One of the Mo's got knocked down and then pulled out a gun. He let off two shoots one skinning one of Donny's friends on the face, and the other one to the clouds. Donny and his friends ran, and the Mo took aim for a third shot, but one of the other ones grabbed him and said, "Are you crazy? Do you know who that is?"

The gunman replied, "I don't give no fuck." One of the other Mo's said, "Fighting is one thing, but if you would have shoot that dude . . . you and your family would have gave a big fuck."

I made it to the zone I see Ronny on the other side with a mad look on his face and red eyes. He was standing next to Charley Paul. Now Charley Paul was a six-foot-one MMA ghetto fighter for the Folks, and Ronny brought him there to use all of his Pokémon powers. He found out the guy that shot the gun last night was named Rome, and he wasn't just one of the Mo's. He was some kinda cousin to our founder; other than that I don't see how Ronny would allow him to keep breathing. Right before the fight started, Ronny told Charley Paul, "I would be very disappointed if this nigga walks away from this fight." Charley Paul replied, "You want me to kill him?" Ronny was silent for a while, then he looked across the circle at me, Twan, and Lil Junior, and said to Charley Paul, "Nawww . . . just make damn sure they carry his ass out that circle."

I looked at Ronny from the other side of the circle and brought back memories. We never faced each other in the circle, and before we were friends, we were rival gang members.

When me and Bangs first saw him he was a couple years older than me, but me and him were about the same size. He was entering the circle facing one of the Mo's that me and Bangs couldn't stand, but this punk was Black Stone so we had to be there. His name was Aron but they called him Ace, he was a big sloppy ass bully and rapist. When Bangs would address him he would say, "What's up, Ass . . . aw, I mean Ace."

I looked across the circle to see Ronny with this mad face and red eyes. Ace was much bigger than him. The circle was where rival gangs would form a fighting ring with their bodies to have one-on-ones. In this circle, it's kill or be killed. With speed, precision, and strength I saw this guy used moves I have never seen before. He busted Ace's eardrum, and maybe castrated him. I don't know—the fight was quick and bloody. It might have taken a minute or two from beginning and the guards getting there. But it was over thirty seconds before they even got there. Ace was laid out on the floor with blood coming from his ear and through his pants from his private part.

There was this Mexican counselor that worked at Jefferson named Mr. Rodriguez. He was one of the good counselors that really cared about the boys there. Jefferson hired all kinds of bad people: we had a racist chairman, burnt-out teachers, abusive guards, and sexual predators everywhere you looked. Mr. Rodriguez ran a detention hall, and he was like none of the above—he was a real good guy. So he had all the hard cases in his class.

He formed a chess club and me, Ronny, and Tyrone Hopkins, aka Lil Ty, became good friends through the game of chess. Lil Ty really wasn't all that little. They called him Lil Ty because he was something like a junior. His mother named him after this guy she liked in high school. She refused to name him after his real father . . . because his name was *Uncle* Gus.

Ty wasn't that much of a fighter either, but he was game. He stood up to any and everybody, so me and Ronny couldn't help but like him even though he was from the west side and a Vice Lord. When Mr. Rodriguez first put us together I thought he' was crazy—he knew I was a Stone, Ronny was a Folks, and this boy was a Vice Lord . . . This shit was just not gonna work."

It was not long after we met that we became real cool. I guess Mr. Rodriguez saw beyond some boy's gang affiliations. After hanging out all the time together, they used to call us the Odd Four: me, Ronny, Ty, and of course Big Bangs.

The Vice Lords were the biggest gang on the west side of the city. So it was pretty odd that a Vice Lord, two Blackstones, and a Gangster became so tight. We all stayed pretty tight even after we left Juvi, but the foursome came to an abrupt end with the death of Bangs, and six months after Lil Ty left Juvi, he was gunned down in a shootout with the police.

Back to the start of the end. Charley Paul beat Rome to a pulp, and now he was on the ground screaming for the Mo's to stop it. Here it goes, me and Twan were about to enter the circle to put an end to the onslaught. Ronny entered also and said, "This is a three-minute fight and it hasn't been three minutes." I said, "Okay you've made your point, but the fight is over . . . CHARLEY PAUL, DID YOU HEAR ME? Let him up."

Then I looked at Ronny with pleading eyes. Ronny gave the okay for Charley Paul to stop cranking on Rome's neck.

Ronny got what he wanted; the Mo's carried Rome out of the circle and rushed him to the ER. Every action has a reaction, and every act of violence begets another act of violence. War was declared at the hospital when the doctor told Rome's teary-eyed grandmother that he will probably never walk again. Grandma breaks down and her cousin comes to console her with a hug. After the consoling Grandma's cousin made a call to the founder of the Blackstone Nation, she just said a few tearful words to her son, "Why did you let this happen?" He tried to say a word edgewise but she said, "Make it right," then she hung up the phone.

One week after the declaration of war at 1:45 a.m., everything changed. It had been raining really hard all night. I was out waiting to meet up with Dorsey, to give him his package. Our inter secret circle took turns paying this fucking cop, and tonight was my turn. I didn't think about it at the time, but it did seem a little funny because on this night he was late, and this greedy ass punk was never late.

At1:46 a.m., Ronny pulled up a block away in his gangster mobile to visit this girl named Putt that he was messing around with.

At 1:48 a.m., shots were heard, *boom, boom, boom*! Then I heard tires burning to get away. I quickly ran through the gangway to see what happened. I saw a dark car hit the corner, and a man lying on the street. My heart fell when I saw that gangster Lincoln. I ran to the man . . . and yes, it was Ronny lying on the cold ground with a hole in his face.

At 1:49 a.m., on the other side of the boulevard, a front and back door was kicked, then *boom, boom, boom*!

At 1:49 a.m. and thirty seconds later, a woman lay dead in a bed, and a necked man with a bullet hole in his ass was busting through a second floor window. He hit the ground running and took another bullet to the shoulder as he picked up the pace. Now he was picking them up and putting them down, and he was gone.

At 2:52 a.m at the hospital, the doctor came out and pronounced Ronny dead. His mother let out an eerie scream that chilled my spine. It shouldn't have because I'm sure I made plenty of mothers make that same sound. Donny consoled his mother.

By 3:00 a.m., the hospital was full of Gangster disciples, and many more were on their way. Main told Twan and Lil Junior to get me because we were about to go. He told Big Don that it was no longer safe, and he should leave also. I told Lil Junior I wasn't leaving. Main came over where we were, and I told him that I didn't care if Larry Hover himself walked in. I was staying right here with Ronny's family.

My oldest friend was lying in the next room cold . . . and I needed to know who put him there. At that time, I didn't know anything about what had happened to Charley Paul. All I knew was something was very familiar about that car that sped off.

The next day, everybody in Motown were on high alert. I found out what happened to Charley Paul. Now we were at war. The Folks blamed the Blackstones for Ronny's death. I wasn't totally sure that they were wrong. Even then, I knew it wasn't a typical Blackstone hit, and something just wasn't right with the whole deal. Within the next couple of days, I talked to Donny, and he didn't think so either. We both thought that Charley Paul had some answers, but no one had seen or heard from him since that awful night.

Most of the time when a hitter or a head gets killed, it was sanctioned by his own people, but in this case nobody knew nothing. I had my suspicions, and it matched with Donny's . . . or so we thought.

Ronny's death was the beginning of the blood war between Motown and No Love. People were dropping like flies; every other day, someone was getting shot. After about two months of kidnaping and torturing to gather information on who killed Ronny and why, I had all the faces.

It started from just a look. One old lady looked at another old lady, and felt all of her little cousin's pain. There were tears . . . A teary-voiced old lady pleaded with her powerful son for vengeance. Next was disappointment. A son, with hurt in his heart, explained to his mother why he can't retaliate and that it can't go any further. Unacceptable decision. A police officer came to an old lady's house, and she handed him an envelope of money. Later that night, an unmarked police car sped from a crime scene. At the same time, a door was getting kicked in and assholes and elbows learned how to fly.

One envelope full of money resulted in a young man getting pronounced dead on arrival, and made another butt-necked man hit the ground running. A second envelope two days later brought a manhunt, a police car trunk, and an escort to their final destination.

This revenge war had so many casualties. What was I gonna do, take revenge on a misguided heartbroken old woman that loved her grandson? I wished someone loved me like that. I told Main what really happened. He was nervous that I would do something. I assured him that it was over, but that wasn't entirely true. The old lady was in the clear, but that son of a bitch that took that envelope had laid the last straw.

It was hot out and the kids had the fire hydrant on. It was around seven because it was starting to get dark. I saw Dorsey coming up the boulevard. I knew he would come to the court way to pick up his regular package from the Mo's.

That night, I decided to give him a little something extra. I waited until he pulled up to the back of the gangway. Everybody was acting normal because they didn't know what was about to go down. As the shorty was coming out to make the drop, I stepped out of the shadows. That cop saw me, but he was too fat and slow, and in a blink of an eye it was over.

I shot him five times point-blank. He yelled out once and started gasping for air. His hands started tugging on his chest. He looked at me and we had eye contact. He stopped grabbing at his chest, his arm slowly dropped to his side as his breathing slowed. I bent over and whispered his wife and kid's name. Right before I put a bullet in his head, I uttered his address . . . BOOM!

All that extra I did, and still this guy didn't die. He lived to testify against me in court. He was no longer bothering the brothers. He was still a cop, but that nip it in the bud shit worked like a motherfucker.

The brothers were right, I shouldn't have shot him. If you do shoot a cop, you better make damn sure that he didn't live, and that there were no witnesses around. It doesn't matter if it's your boy, your girl, or even your mama. If they got caught, they will be at your trial to testify against you.

Those people just don't play when it comes to shooting one of them. They gave me four life sentences. The judge said to me, "Young man, you will do eighty years before you step foot on the street again. You'll be an old man and I'll be dead and gone, but I won't lose one night of sleep over it . . . Animals like you need to be in a cage."

I stood there with a stern look on my face and a gangster stare as though that was going to change my outcome. But underneath my pants I was shaking out of control. This old white man in a black robe sitting ten feet high looked down at me and said, "Do you have anything to say?"

At that moment, I pictured myself as an old slave in chains. The thought uttered my silence. My mouth would not open, so I just shook my head no.

"Bailiff, take him away!"

Those words echoed in my head so loud, it gave me a splitting headache.

I said to myself, "At least I'm out of the county." Now that everything had come to the light, everything has turned to hell. The heads sent out hits on us. Twan was killed about three weeks after I went to jail. I think Main and Lil Junior were down south somewhere. They sent a couple of dudes to me in the county. I knew they wish they wouldn't have followed orders. So to say I was glad to get out of the county and go to prison was an understatement.

Chapter 7

Back Home

I arrived at Louis Ville State Correctional facility.

As I walked through the gated corridor, my mind started to ease. There were guys talking stuff, making threats, some even showing their private parts. I stayed in that strait line carrying my gear. Someone from the upper decks screamed out, "You gonna be my bitch." I closed my eyes and looked up with a smile because it brought back the first day I walked into Jefferson Boys' Home. I opened my eyes and my shoulders got broader, my chest was bigger, my stare was colder, my heartbeat was steady and calm. I was home.

The first couple of months were a little hard with having to prove yourself to everybody, and finding a clique. I wasn't Blackstone on the books anymore, but I was in my heart. Hell that kinda stuff didn't matter in this place, anyway. If you thought you faced segregation and prejudice on the streets, you don't know segregation and prejudice. It's all about the race here—the white with the whites, the black with the blacks, and so on. And inside of that you find your clique—you know, the few guys inside your race you grove with.

My best buddy up in there was Abbot; the problem was he's kind of a loner. He's a black Puerto Rican Jew, I call him Juan Epstein. He got that nickname from me because he is a Puerto Rican Jew like the character on "Welcome back, Carter"; besides he was tougher than a motherfucker.

The black government had a lot of rules in here. I was young and wild, so I wasn't trying to follow none of them. The heads would try to keep me in line, but they couldn't. Normally when you get out of line with the heads here, you wake up dead. In this place it was more young and wild than it was old and wise, and more and more of us were coming every day. Eighty percent of the young and wild looked to me for guidance. Now I never been no head or leader, so I didn't challenge the rule. There was one thing for sure and two things for certain—I couldn't be touched. Yeah, on this plantation, I was the young black straw boss, the guards were Massa, and the white Aryans ran the guards.

I remember when I first met Abbot. A few of the guys were talking about what brought them here. I told them about how I emptied a six-shot revolver into a cop, but I didn't tell them why a revolver. The revolver was the first gun I ever had. Now everybody knows that I always carry two black pear-handle forty-five autos. Three days later this black Puerto Rican Jew walked up to me in the laundry room and said, "Hey, what's up man. You know your story was a little strange to me."

After I looked at him like he lost his mind, I said, "Dude...what are you talking about."

He said, "It's one thing in your story that's bothering me."

I looked at him as though, "Oh shit, this boy is crazy."

He saw the way I was looking at him, so he took a step back and said, "I don't mean you no harm, but for the life of me I can't figure out why you shoot him with a thirty-eight."

I looked at him for a second or two, then I put my hand up to my mouth. We were the only ones in the laundry room at that time. I said to him, "You are the first person to ever ask me that." It didn't even come up in my trial. So I decided to tell him.

I told him about the day I walked away from Jefferson. I can't say I broke out and ran away because remember, no one chased after me. Our conversation took me to how I walked through at least eight different neighborhoods. I was almost at my cousin Main's house, but I had one more hood to go through . . . yes, No Love.

I didn't really understand the boundaries or how dangerous going through all these hoods was. I never had turf wars on the streets or fought a rival gang member for being in my hood. Remember, I've been incarcerated all my life, and I got blessed into the gang life in the inside. This was my first breath of free air since I left my mom as a little kid.

Well, almost at the end of my journey, I ran into a couple of guys. I didn't even see nobody because I wasn't really paying attention until I heard whistles from behind me down the street. I looked across the street, and it was a whole group of dude. I guess that whistle was to let them know I was there. When they started looking over at me, I knew I was about to get a crash course in that turf shit.

Somebody in the crowd said, "Who the fuck is that?" I must admit his tone did worry me a little bit. There were a lot of them and they started walking toward me. I couldn't run because they were standing between me and Motown. So I started devising a strategy on how I would fight them, and in every calculation, I ended up at the back of an ambulance.

I took a big breath, and I thought about what Bangs would say to me right now. "Whatever you do, just make damn sure you're not the only one leaving in an ambulance." He would've given me that look and then a smile and say, "Hey! If they come for the bull, give them the fucking horns!"

I braced myself for pain, then balled my fist tightly, and quickly stepped toward them. I stopped when I heard a familiar voice and phrase . . . "My Nigga!"

Ronny walked out of the group and said, "Boy, what are you doing around here?" I was really happy to see this dude, and I'm putting emphasis on *happy*.

He told the other Folks, "Be cool that's my people." They went back across the street and he walked over to me. He said, "I saw you when you first hit the block. I chilled to see what you was going to do . . . I saw you soldier up and prepare to go ham." He shook my hand and gave me a man hug, then he said, "You still 'bout it . . . But check this out, little bro, these streets ain't like that—you got to arm yourself if you gonna stay alive out here." He opened his coat and took out a black steel 9 millimeter. He could tell by the way I looked at it I never had a gun. So he quickly let it be known that he wasn't giving it to me. Then he took out an old rust thirty-eight.

He said, "This gun is a piece of shit, but hey, it's your piece of shit . . . All you got to do is point and pull." So I thought it was poetic justice that I killed the police that killed Ronny with the gun Ronny gave me.

That was the beginning of our friendship. In this place, you need friends, but you need loyalty more. With my man Abbot, I had both. We were alike only because both of us were criminals, but that was the end of our similarities. I was just a common thug, but Abbot, he was some kinda Mater mind—this dude was smart as hell. He received a college degree in finance at the age of twenty. He wanted to work at the stock market, but the boys at the market frowned on that black Puerto Rican Jew thing. So he got a job in a grocery store and sent out resumes once a week for three years. Between that time, life got a little bigger. He got married, had two kids, and one was on the way.

Once he got the news that he was about to be responsible for another mouth, he realized he couldn't stay as an honest upstanding American citizen and be able to feed his family. When poor black people from the hood need money and turn to crime, it's normally some type of drug thing. Not my man, Abbot. He devised a plan to rob a bank.

That's big time . . . some real white-boy shit. This dude robbed five banks over a four-year span before he was caught. They never could prove he was involved in the bank robberies, so he got ten years for hitting a police officer with a car. He used to joke and say, "I got a fifty-fifty deal, five years for hitting the cop and five years for suspicion." Then he would laugh. Whenever he tells his story and laugh at the end, people would say, "Man, what the hell are you laughing about . . . you're in jail." He would say to them, "I'm gonna laugh now and when I get out . . . hell, I'm going to have the last laugh."

People just thought he was crazy, but I knew why he laughed. They never did find that money.

For four and a half years we taught one another and shared each other stories, but mainly that was one-sided. I might have shared in the story telling, but the teaching was all his.

He taught me how to really read—you know, the comprehension and understanding part. Through his stories and letters from his family, I got to live a whole other life. Now it's here, Abbot's big day finally came. He's going to be released, and I knew this day was coming for a while. I'm happy for him but sad for me because I'm about to lose my friend and inspiration. I had friends before that I loved and lost permanently. My connection with Abbot was no stronger than my connection with Bangs, just different. Every other friend or associate that I ever had in my life were just like me, but this guy was from another planet. For starters, he had a wife and kids, mother and father, a sister and two brothers, who loved him deeply.

They wrote him all the time, and he would let me read the letters, even some of the personal ones. I would read those letters and think of my mother in a different way . . . what if . . .

We said our goodbyes and that was that. We didn't entertain the fantasy of what we would do when I got out because we both knew this was my last residence. One week after he left, I received a letter and pictures, and that continued every week for five and a half months. The letters stopped coming, and after a while I stopped writing.

A year later, a guy from Abbot's neighborhood came in. I asked about my friend. He told me Abbot got killed in a robbery six months after he got out. Some sixteen-year-old boy wanted his watch and robbed him. That night, I cried like a baby. I even thought about ending it all. Thinking of nipping myself in the bud wasn't nothing new. It wasn't just because of the news about Abbot. I had people die in my life. It always comes to, at the end of the day, good or bad, it still was My Life.

During that time, I was giving life a lot of thought. I was in my late twenties, and I've been locked up most of my life. I never had a real girlfriend. I only had two visitors since I got here. One was from my cousin Main, and the other one was from Donny, and that was when I first got here. Looking on the bright side, there's still time for people to come and visit. I got over seventy more years to go.

There is a God, surely. Because nine years, six months, fourteen days and two and a half hours of me being locked up at Louis Ville State Correctional, I met with a lawyer. This lawyer was a public defender, but he gave me some news worthy of a thousand-dollar-an-hour attorney. Everything came out on Dorsey, that cop I shot. The district attorney has dismissed all the cases he was involved in. At first,

I didn't understand what all that had to do with me, until this fantastic lawyer told me I was getting out in a day or two.

When they took me back to my cell, I was so excited. Once the cell door shut, I became scared and sad. It started to dawn on me that I didn't know what to do outside these walls. I had no one waiting for me. I didn't even have anyone in particular that was happy I was getting out. I started thinking about all the stuff I missed out on, like never having a job, never going to a regular high school, not finishing high school, and I have never even had a puppy love.

Here it was, almost ten years later, and I was out of jail and not on parole. I was twenty-nine years old with no education, no money, and no hope. Are you paying attention to this multigenerational pattern? Without no prospects I had to go back to what I knew—the streets and the drug game. I went back to Motown to try to pick up where I left off.

Time does not wait for no man. It was a new game, with new players. About two years after I got locked up, Daddy Keith, the head general in No Love, was caught in a drive by while picking up his kids from school. Keith and his fourteen-year-old lay dead and the twelve-year-old son would spend the rest of his life in a wheelchair.

A year after that, the federal government thought it was a good idea to get rid of gangs by rounding up all the heads of all gangs and lock them up. Now when you first think about it, you say, "Oh well, these were bad people. They controlled the streets and the drug game. They decided who got killed. They corrupted our youth and controlled them."

I wondered if this was by design or did the government really drop the ball. If you remove all the chiefs the Indians will go awry. To say the streets was in anarchy was a fucking understatement. Lil Pooky and them went butt-fucking wild, with no guidance, no consequences, or repercussions—it was open season on everybody and anybody. It seems to me that all the government did was create thousands of Franky Bs . . . and that can't be good.

I was back in the old hood and I couldn't find any faces I knew, and when I did they were all strung-out on drugs. Even Mrs. Jones was gone; she was the lady with all the kids and everybody used to hang out at her house. Now it was just a vacant lot.

I just kept walking around the old neighborhood, hoping to see a familiar face. I asked anybody I saw that might be a user or seller, where was the drug spots? I saw this prostitute that looked real familiar to me, so I walked over to her. The closer I got, the more familiar she looked to me.

When I got up to her, I said, "Anne?" She knew me right off. She gave me this great big hug, then she said, "What's been up with you?"

I said, "I'm hanging in there." I told her I just got out of jail, then I said, "What a coincidence, just the other day I saw Andre. I asked him about you, he told me he runs into you now and then. He was doing a real good, he's working over at the youth center. He asked me if I needed a job, but I'm not into all that nine-to-five shit, if you know what I mean."

She said, "Honey, I know exactly what you mean. Every time I see him, he tries to get me to change my ways and get a job." I told her that Ms. Pack was in the hospital from alcohol poisoning. She said, "What, man, that's messed up. You seen her?"

"Naw, I haven't seen her in years. Andre told me, they keep in touch."

She said, "I'm going to try to get over there to see her, she was always cool with me, especially after she adopted Andre. She is going to be alright, right?"

"I really don't know I didn't go into it too deep with him."

She said in this sad voice, "Man, that's messed up. I didn't even think she drank."

Then I asked her, "What was up with Tony, and baby Joddy?"

She said, "Tony's been dead for over five years now. He got shot down on the low-end fucking with somebody. I can't believe you remember baby Jody, she's not no baby no more. She's just as cute as she wanted to be, and *smaaart*. She is doing a really good. She's living with my grandmother. Baby girl is a straight A student. She graduated from high school top of her class, and she's goes to Duke University on a full academic scholarship."

I said, "Damn that's good, and that's really good how you keep up with her."

Then she said something that surprised me. She said that Jody was her blood sister. I never knew that. "It sure was nice seeing you, but I have to get out of here," I said.

She replied, "Give me your number."

I told her I didn't have one. She said, "Me neither." So she gave me a hug and said, "You take care of yourself."

As I was walking away, she asked me if I could loan her ten bucks, I said, "Man, I'm broke as a joke."

Then she said, "I'll hook you up for it." She meant some kind of sexual favor. I really was broke, besides she was the closest thing I had to a sister. I was staying in this hotel down on 39th street. That dump was costing me forty bucks a day. I was running out of the little money I had from prison. See, I wasn't fortunate enough to be on parole, where you have to stay in a halfway house, someone make you get a job, and monitored your every move. I had to figure out how to make some money, and soon. It got so bad that I looked at Andre's business card a time or two, and afterward I would laugh and say to myself, "Nigga, you better man the fuck up."

The next day, I went back to Motown, determined to find some work. The word around the hood was, this guy named T had the biggest crew, and they were making money, so he was the man to see. I told him who I was. It was something in his eyes that made me feel like he knew me already. Then he said with a smile,

"What's up, you don't remember me, do you? I'm Lil T, I used to run with the shorties, when you were around here."

I said, "Damn, I do remember you, but check this out, I just got out of the joint. I could sure use a blessing, and you're just the man that could do it."

He said, "What's up, Mo, how can I aid and assist you."

"I need you to front me for something, so I can get back on."

He said, "Before we do any business, I got to ask you something. You're not fucking with that shit, are you?"

I got this offended look on my face, then I said, "Nall, Mo, I don't go that route."

Then he got real serious, and walked right up to me, and said, "Humor me, and open your eyes up real wide." He looked for a second then he smiled, and said, "I got you, Mo, my newcomers get 30 percent. I'll give you 35 percent since you are old school."

Yeah, he had me alright, he had me as a tester, selling nickel bags to new customers. They did that in case the person was an undercover cop or some kind of informant. The Mo's start all the young guys off as testers. They do that for two reasons: one, it helps them to build new clientele. Two, if they are the police, they would only catch him with one nickel bag. The kid would get very little, if any time in jail, and the cop's undercover career would be over.

I knew I shouldn't take the chance of being a tester. If I got caught, I was looking to do some serious time. I didn't want to go back to jail, but he said that was all he had right now. I knew that was a lie. That nigger was trying to test me, and make me pay some dues. Though he knew, I've been tough tested years ago. I've paid my dues before some of them were even born. I knew if I sold to new customers, sooner or later, I would get caught. If I got caught, it wasn't going to be a slap on the wrist. I was going to do at least ten long years in the joint.

I had to think of another way to make money. I decided the Blackstones didn't care nothing about me. If they did, they wouldn't have left me with no way out. I had no alternative, but to stick the whole crew up. Needless to say, I was not a Blackstone anymore. The whole messed-up part about it was, his crew only had two thousand and some change. I could have sworn, I saw them with tens of thousands, maybe my eyes were playing tricks on me. Maybe it was the way they were out there fronting like they had something. Whatever the reason was that I thought these punks had lute, I was wrong. When it was all over, I was left with just a couple thousand made to look like more. Oh yeah, as for little T, I gave him a crash course on Big Bangs's "nip that in the bud." That little money I took off them didn't go real far.

Chapter 8

Slow Day, Fast Night

I went to live on the west side with one of my cousins—a déjà vu. I hope you haven't forgotten our family motto or should I say model because we damn sure shaped ourselves to it: no education, no money, and no hope. My cousins lived up to the family model very well. Some of them went way beyond it; to call them niggers was like a step-up. There are exceptions to every rule as one of my cousins on my father's side actually had potential.

His name was Deon, but we all called him DaDa. This boy was real nice-looking and pretty smooth. He was everybody's favorite. People in the neighborhood loved him, especially the girls. DaDa was five years younger than me, and I've been in jail forever so we weren't that close. He still reached out to me when I told him my situation.

This boy could have made it to the NBA. He was on the right track. In his freshman and sophomore years in high school, he averaged almost twenty points in the varsity team. In the summer between his sophomore and junior year, he was invited to play in the annual All-Stars of high school versus the All-Stars of college game. That's when everyone knew for sure he was NBA material. He put up a triple double, with forty points, ten rebounds, and fourteen assists. His junior year was off the hook, he was averaging thirty-seven points and sixteen rebounds a game. After the end of the season, it seemed as if every scout in the country was trying to talk to him, even some NBA scouts. e

In a blink of an eye the scouts stopped coming, the phone stopped ringing, and the crowd stopped cheering. All because in a frozen moment in time, a seventeen-year-old boy picked up a gun and pulled the trigger.

DaDa did two long years in prison for one second of bad judgment. Again there were two reports—the official police report and the street report. The courts called it attempted murder, but the word on the streets was, it was simply self-defense.

Although jail was a dreadful place to be, it was not a total waste. I mean he did learn how to be vicious, and he picked up a bad drug habit. I guess he needed those tools just to cope with everyday life behind bars. If you ever spent any significant time in jail, you would know it leaves you with a life-lasting experience.

I know in my heart, jail and everything that goes with it is bad. I must admit, it got to be something good about going to jail when you're from the ghetto. How else can you explain this? It seemed like to me, people were so happy that he had come from jail. Not so much that he had got released, but it was like a badge of honor that he had gone to jail and did his time.

When DaDa got out of jail, he kinda picked up from where he left off, of course, his basketball career was over. The girls still flocked to him like he was the Fonz. I guess people in general flocked to him.

Chapter 9

First Love

One day we went over to one of his girls' house to pick up some money. He introduced me to her and her sister. I remember it like it was yesterday, this beautiful girl, with this soft angel voice who reached her hand out to me, and said, "Hi, my name is Tosha. I'm Deb's sister."

She had long beautiful brown hair and a golden complexion. She had to be close to six feet tall because she was just an inch or two shorter than me. I lost myself for a minute, as I was looking almost eye to eye with this mesmerizing green-eyed goddess.

DaDa and his girl, her sister, went into the back room. It was okay because I had her to keep me company. We had a pretty good conversation. I even managed to make her laugh a few times. She was so fine, I could hardly believe it when she said, "Can I see you again"?

After hearing those words I was gone, I was in love. And it wasn't just because she was beautiful, it was the first time in my life that someone actually wanted to see me just because they liked me. After that day, we had been seeing a lot of one another.

Two days after meeting her, she called me and said to come over. I got a little scared because I heard something in her voice. I wasn't sure if it was good or bad, but either way I was scared. If it was bad, then she was about to tell me that she made a mistake and I wasn't good enough to be with her. On the other hand, if it was *good*, now that terrified me. I didn't have a lot of experience with women, and what if I mess up so bad that she would laugh in my face.

The arrival . . . I was at the front door contemplating ringing the bell or not. The door suddenly opened and all my fears were chased away by this big beautiful smile, baby-soft hand touch, and angel voice saying, "Boy, get in here."

She walked me through the house straight to her bedroom, never releasing my hand. Every step I took, my heart was beating fast. Once we made it to the bed, my heart stopped altogether. With her arms tightly around me and a passionate kiss, my heartbeat was in sync with hers. As we lay back on those cloth sheets together, we magically transformed ourselves into synchronized swimmers.

Our clothes were off and I saw her, and she saw me. In that moment, it was a religious experience. It was the most beautiful thing I have ever seen or heard of. First penetration was like the show "Love American Style"—all I saw were big bright blue and white lights . . . explosion in one second . . . But we had the whole night and every day after.

She wasn't just a girlfriend—she was my better half, the Yin to my Yang. By hanging out with her, I started to change. She taught me how to forgive others and myself. I was more tolerant of people in general, and for once I saw the good in life. I was no longer the vicious animal I've been all my life. I moved in with Tosha two weeks after we met. She got me to stop street life, and I even got a job at the neighborhood supermarket. It seemed as though I was breaking our family tradition.

We had a wonderful life, but being who I was, I always had doom at the back of my mind. We had been together about four months, and she called me from work to ask me to meet her at the park. I saw her sitting on the bench, under this big tree where we always sat. I walked up to her, she stood up, and gave me a hug and a kiss.

Then she said, "Sit down, I have something to talk to you about."

I saw the seriousness in her eyes. I said to myself, all good things has to come to an end. Then I said, "I know, it's over, right?"

She kind of looked at me as though she was a little mad or surprised at what I said. As she was looking at me with those beautiful eyes, she said, "Franky, don't say another word . . . I love you every day with all my heart, and I'm two months pregnant."

I loved this girl, I loved the idea of having a good loving family, but I knew I couldn't trust it. The shit that's in my blood, my DNA, was not right. I came from bad stock. But for months she made me forget that.

Tosha wasn't all pure. She and her sister hung out with my cousin. My cousin had very bad drug habits. It seemed to me that all his friends got high in one way or another, and my lovely, beautiful goddess was no different. She didn't smoke the pipe; her drug of choice was max.

That's where you roll a joint up with cocaine in it. Tosha thought she was better than other people that did drugs because she only did drugs occasionally.

Chapter 10

Family Tradition

It wasn't long before I was smoking it too. I knew better, I mean I saw what drugs did to people up close. I sold them and now I'm buying them. What a turn of events. We stayed together until our baby was six months old. By the time we were breaking up, we both had pretty bad habits. I wasn't into that max thing; I went straight to the pipe.

One night, we were all getting high, in the basement of DaDa's house. The nigger that had the drugs was acting kind of funny. He was being very generous, especially to the women. This guy was normally stingy as hell, but not tonight. DaDa didn't pay too much attention to what was going on. I did, and I knew why he was being so free-hearted. He wanted to get up with my woman, and as I think about it now, I believe she was game for it. I wasn't game for shit. I started to "nip him in the bud" and take his stash.

DaDa told me to chill, then he said, "Don't trip, big F, we're going to get our own shit."

It was that nigger's lucky day, we just put his ass out. He was mad when DaDa told him to leave. This punk was acting like DaDa did something wrong to him. I don't think he even realized that my little cousin saved his life that night.

We went looking for a vic, that's short for victim, you know somebody to rob. Now we were about to embark on a real tricky game. Whenever you rob somebody, you better be prepared to kill them. A stick up can turn into a murder quicker than a heartbeat. DaDa was not a coward—he would fight and all, and even burst your fucking head. Shooting somebody and murder . . . that wasn't really DaDa's thing, so I wondered if I should take him to do this. DaDa and his addiction insisted that we go, and my need for the next pull on the pipe concurred this bad idea.

We came up on this nigger walking down the street. We ran up on him and grabbed this punk, but this boy wasn't nothing nice. He put up a pretty good fight. Once we got him on the ground, he tried to scream. My cousin pulled out this big-ass roscoe and cocked the trigger back. You know, he shut what they call . . . the fuck up.

As we were catching our breath, I asked my cousin, "Why in the hell didn't you pull that thing out at first? I got a damn knot on my head, and your lip is busted. I wish I could have known you had it, my man would have had to deal with all six of these hot ones."

After all that, if you didn't count that nigger's bus card, he was as broke as us. We let him go and decided that the night wouldn't be a total waste. We used his bus card and went downtown. We saw a fat one, there he was, the perfect vic. It was this well-dressed white guy coming out this bar. He was middle-aged, slightly overweight, and sloppy drunk. We waited until he tried to get in his car. He was fumbling with his keys,

He was about to drive drunk, so the way I looked at it, we were doing him a service.

DaDa walked up to him and said, "Excuse me sir, but do you have the time?" As he rolled his sleeve back to look at his watch. I came up from the back and hit him in the head with a brick. I think that's when I first realized something was seriously wrong with me, because as this man was out cold, I had the urge to hit him again.

DaDa stopped me by saying, "This is a good score, don't mess it up by giving us a murder charge. Look, Franky, this fool got mad cash on him, credit cards, and jewelry." We took all the cash and jewelry; my cousin told me to leave the credit cards, but I was stupid and took them anyway. All the cash was gone the same night. We sold the jewelry the next day. By the next night, I was broke. I decided to do something really stupid. I tried to use the credit cards once the money and jewelry were all gone. I felt even stronger about not throwing the cards away.

When I tried to use those cards I got caught, but it could have been a lot worse. I was going to charge some merchandize to one of the cards. The cashier told me that she couldn't accept the card. I was okay with that, but then she said she couldn't return it either. I was about to give her a crash course in Big Bangs Philosophy 101. Before I was able to do anything, the police were there. It seems as though this cashier wasn't as dumb as I thought. She informed the police about the card even before she told me.

Chapter 11

Coming Home Again

Another Saturday morning I woke up in custody. I was sober enough to understand I was facing some more serious time. But at least for the weekend I was going to be here at the county. And what do you know, I saw Lil T and some of the Mo's. They stared from across the room. About this time, I was going through real bad withdrawals and was in no mood to play no games. It reminded me of a lion that ran into a pack of wild dogs; they were many but the lion was fierce. They wouldn't even make eye contact; they stayed on their side of the room like pups with their tails tucked between their legs.

On Monday morning, I stood with hands shaking before a man in a black robe. I wasn't shaking from fear, it was from withdrawal of drugs. I looked up at this man as though he was the lion, and I was the pup with his tail between his legs. I don't remember the whole speech the judge gave once they found me guilty. I do still remember those key words he said, "Menace and terror to society." And right before he dropped that mighty gavel down, I heard the loudest words that came out of his mouth: "Twenty years."

For the first time in my life, I was worried about going to jail. It wasn't the fear of being locked up; it was the fear of missing out on things here in the world. Flashes of swimming in the bedsheet with Tosha went through my mind, even though we broke up for a while. After my mom and before Tosha, I never let myself want or need anything. I've been in and out of jail all my life, but this time it was different . . . I valued my freedom, so this one hurt.

Yep, you don't miss it until you can't have it anymore.

As I looked back on that time, I was sure it was the drugs doing all my thinking for me. Whenever drugs were your top advisers, you will make bad decisions.

The bus ride *home* was a long one. We stopped at two other prisons to pick up and drop off other prisoners. Until the first stop, I was sitting by myself in the front row left side window seat. The guards gathered up four prisoners for drop-off and returned with five. The first inmate of the bus was Marvin Moncrete, a six-foot-three, four-hundred-pound smelly blabbermouth. And they sat him right next to me.

So for one hour and forty minutes of our acquaintance, he told me a lifetime information about himself. The man even told me the nickname his mother calls him, "Mammoth Moncrete." We pulled into the next prison, and a guard called out the names of three prisoners that were getting off. Once he said, "Moncrete," I yelled out "Thank God!" and he looked at me with a frown. I said as they were hauling his big ass off the bus, "Hey, big man, don't take it personal, but take it easy." I had a smirk on my face until they rolled him on the bus.

The Tin Man. That's what everybody called him. I knew he was coming on the bus because Moncrete told me. What I didn't know was they were bringing him on the bus strapped to a two-wheel dolly with a Hannibal Lecter mask on. And you know they strapped him in on the front row, left.

They had him muzzled and tied down so tight the only thing he could move were his eyes. And he moved those eyes . . . directly toward me. It kind of freaked me out because I've never seen anyone bound like that.

He kept staring so I looked back at him and said, "Hey, did you know Moncrete has some cousins that live around here." I didn't say nothing mean; why make another enemy? I have enough of them in here already. Some inmates that I've wronged in one way or another and every single guard in here. Whenever I get stopped by police and they run my name through the system, it pops up COP SHOOTER and boy, do they get mad and go on alert. I guess my file don't say the cop I shot was a dirty, ruthless gangbanger himself.

Roy Ray Duncan Jr. aka the Tin Man. You know, they put him in a cell with me. Turned out old Tin Man wasn't a bad guy after all. They transferred him here because he got in a fight with two inmates. Even though one of the guys lost an eye, and the other one, it's probably safe to say he won't be making anymore babies, that wasn't the reason why they transferred him. One of the guards that was breaking up the fight ran up from the back, Roy turned and elbowed him so hard that his helmet and face mask flew off. As the other guards were restraining his arms, he lunged and bit the helmetless guard on the nose and ripped it off. As they beat and stomped him, he chewed and swallowed.

After that the guard retired; people called him bone nose. You are probably saying that was messed up and the guard was just doing his job, but sometimes he did a little more. Sergeant Keiffer was a piece of gay shit, he would make some of the new young guys that was a little scared suck his dick for protection. But I thought his job was to protect them . . . hey, but what do I know, I'm just an inmate.

Jail does serve a purpose—it's a place where people that do bad things go. If you ask me the Tin Man was displaced. He should not have been in jail in the first place. Roy Ray Duncan was just an old country boy from Mississippi that obeyed the law. He didn't have so much as a speeding ticket before his forty-ninth birthday. Now he was fifty and his record had four murders, three attempted murders, and multiple bodily harm charges.

Me and Tin Man were pretty close; he was like a father figure to me. At first it was hard for him to get through to me. Remember, I came in here with a hundred-dollar-a-day habit and that not a monkey . . . it was a fucking gorilla on my back. With Tin Man being who he was and not a natural animal, he helped nurtured me back to the living until he was able to pull the gorilla off my back. Withdrawal is a mothafucka, and going through it in jail can be a death sentence.

So yes, the Tin Man saved a worthless life and shaped it into a decent life. He taught me how to stand up as a man without violence and a gun. He taught me it didn't matter what family I was born into, and my actions determine my worth. And like all close inmates we did share the story of what brought us here. I told him my story, and he told me his story. Before I heard his story, I knew he was different, but after I heard it, I knew he was a hero.

All this foolery started with Johnny Brubaker's nephew, Henry Washington, but everybody was calling him Lil L. I don't know how they got L from Henry or Washing, but he was little maybe about five foot ten, one hundred and thirty pounds. Henry was one of those mixed kids, you know the one with the light eyes and the wavy hair, the real petty boy type. He was twenty-one and down here from Chicago with a shiny fast car. So you know all these small-town country girls went wild for the boy, including seventeen-year-old Baby Gwen Duncan.

Roy and Gwen grew up and got married in a one-mile town called Lilliput, Mississippi. He repeated after the preacher at the tender age of eighteen, and she was fifteen years old and six months pregnant when she replied "I Do." One month later Gwen had some complication and gave birth to a premature baby boy. Their son Roy Ray Duncan III lived for six months just long enough to get too attached. Years passed and they thought they couldn't have kids, and along came Baby Gwen. Roy looked at it as a gift from God. He loved and protected that girl something crazy. She was his sidekick whenever you saw him, you saw her. He taught her everything he knew—how to fish, fight, play basketball, and football. They used to play chest outside the corner store on weekends. By the end of her junior year in high school, the topic of their conversation was always the college she would attend and the plans for her bright future.

That summer things were changing. They didn't hang out as much. They played chest only one time the whole summer. His sidekick was gone, but he just chalked it up as she was growing up and needed her space. By the beginning of her senior year, the big changes started to appear, like the makeup. The expensive sexy clothing that Roy didn't buy. The new crowd she was hanging out with, the fancy fast car with the Illinois license plates that he had seen her get out of on more than one occasion.

She was eighteen now and about to graduate from high school, her grades slipped a lot that last year but some colleges were still interested. The problem was she was not interested in them. A couple of weeks before graduation, she broke her parents heart. She told them that she was taking a year off to find herself, and she was in love with Lil L. She said she and Mary Ann were going to Chicago to be in Lil L's rap video. Mary Ann and Baby Gwen had been friends since kindergarten.

A father struggles hard with news like that. But with her being his miracle child, he gave her whatever she wanted, including her freedom. The first couple of weeks she called a few times. The third week her parents saw on Facebook pictures and the rap video she was in. Baby

Gwen and her father had a falling out over Lil L and the provocative nature of the video. She said to her dad, "I love this man, and you are just jealous of the money my man is making."

After hearing his baby girl that he gave the world to, say those words to him, he replied with some harsh words of his own. There was silence. And then a strong high pitch, "I hate you!" and a fast reply, "I hate you too!"

Silence, and then "Baby, I'm so—"

Click.

Click was not just the sound of a phone hanging up, it was also the sound of his hopes and dreams saying goodbye.

He had seen her about two months after the *click*; she was downtown with that worthless Lil L, Maryann, a couple of other guys, and some sleazy-looking women.

Baby Gwen and her father picked up where the click left off. They had a big public falling out, and with the harsh words he had to say about his daughter in front of the town, people started calling him Tin Man because they said he didn't have a heart, but he did. It was just in pieces.

Over the next two years, they heard from their daughter maybe five times.

It was seven thirty in the evening and the phone rang. Roy answered.

MARYANN (Whispers)
Hello, Mr. Duncan . . . This is Maryann . . .

ROY
Maryann, what's wrong, where's Baby Gwen?
Roy heard someone in the background.

VOICE
Bitch, didn't I tell you ass not to be on the phone.

MARYANN

Gwen is in trouble and she needs you!

CLICK!

He screamed out, "GWEN!" at the same time he pushed the redial button. As she ran up saying, "What's wrong?" he heard a busy tone. He told his wife what Maryann said to him, and what happened. They tried to redial again and the same outcome. They started to dial every number they have on their daughter and Maryann, but none were working.

He told her to keep trying as he grabbed his jacket and headed straight for Ruth Anne's house, Maryann's mother. When he got there, she wasn't home, so he headed to the only other place she would be. He made it there in record time, to Jimmy's Bar, a little hole in the wall tavern. There she was at the end of the bar, drinking by herself. By the time he got there, she already had one too many.

She saw Roy walking toward her, she quickly downed her drink, and her eyes swelled up with tears as she saw the seriousness in his face. She shouted, "What's wrong? Did something happen to Maryann? I knew something bad was going to happen, I just knew it."

Roy said to her, "I don't know what's going on with the girls, but it's not good and something is wrong."

He told her about the call he got from Maryann. She took another drink and in a drunken voice she said, "It was a bad idea from the get go to let them girls follow the devil to Chicago."

Roy said, "Yeah, I know, but that's not why I came to see you. I need to know how to get back in touch with Maryann."

She replied with, "I don't know any more than you about how to get in touch with them . . . What did Baby Gwen say?"

"I didn't get a chance to talk to Baby Gwen before that guy snatched the phone from Maryann and hung up."

In a teary drunk voice Ruth Anne said, "Oh my god, I don't know what we gonna do, my baby needs me."

"The best thing you can do is go home in case Maryann tries to call. I'm going to the police station and make a report," said Roy.

Ruth Anne took a deep breath and seemed to sober up. She said, "No, don't do that. We can call the sheriff from your truck. We need to go see the Brubakers now."

They pulled up to the Brubakers place, and out comes Joyce Brubaker. She said in a rough voice, "What you need around here, Roy Duncan, and who is that with you?"

Ruth Anne got out of the truck and said, "Hey, Joyce. It's Ruth Anne McDonald."

Joyce said, "Seeing you and that drunk around here can only mean one thing . . . So what happened to them girls?"

Ruth Anne said under her breath, "Well hell . . . that ain't that nice."

Joyce Brubaker is a six-foot tough lesbian that's not all there in the head, and known for toting a gun and small weapons of much destruction. So they were a little easy on how they will conduct this news.

Johnny Brubaker came out the house to see what was going on with his sister. Roy told them both everything that went on earlier that night. Johnny wasn't giving us much help. Joyce gave him a look and said, "Tell them whatever you know."

Johnny replied, "I can't say nothing . . . You talking about turning in Zeb's boy." Before Roy could say something, she blurted out, "Zeb son, my ass . . . but so what if he is. Zeb wasn't shit and he is worse . . . Before you open your mouth again think about what if it was one of your girls. I know you keep in touch with him."

Johnny said, "Okay, you know he's in Chicago, he's on the south side of the city. The last mail I got from him had a return address of 6930 E. Parnell. I think that's where he was living, but he got another spot on some street called Ashland. He's making videos out of some old hotel."

Roy said, "I know . . . some type of rap videos."

Johnny kinda dropped his head and said, "They're not all rap videos . . . Some are sex videos."

Roy's worry turned to anger, he didn't give a fuck about Joyce or her weapons. He grabbed Johnny by the collar and said, "So he's making sex videos with my daughter."

Johnny knocked Roy's hands off his collar and said, "What the fuck are you doing? I'm out here helping y'all against my kin . . . I don't know if your daughter's in it. I know he was doing it, and that's all I know."

Roy and Ruth left with that information and a disconnected cell number Joyce gave them. They were heading straight to the police station. They talked to the sergeant on duty, and all he could do was make a call to the Chicago police. The desk sergeant in Chicago said they had to make a missing person report.

Roy dropped off Ruth and told her he will call when he make it to Chicago. He was back home with his wife telling her everything that went on, all while packing a bag.

He saw a sign that read Chicago 735 miles; he stepped on the gas. After eight hours and forty-five minutes of demolishing the speed limit, he came to a sign that read "Welcome to Chicago."

He made it to the police station and told them everything. They informed him that all he can do was to fill out a missing person report, and in twenty-four hours they will make a wellness visit. Before he could say another word, Roy was out the door.

He arrived at 6930 E. Parnell the address Johnny gave him. The bell had Johnson on it but no one came to the door. As Roy was banging on the door, he shouted his daughter's name at the windows. The next door neighbor came out of the house. She asked, "What are you doing screaming like that at this time in the morning?"

With red teary eyes, Roy said, "I'm sorry, but it is very important that I talk to the people that live here."

The neighbor can see in Roy's face that he was desperate and scared. Her mannerism and tone changed. She said, "What's wrong, sir . . . where are my manners? My name is Gladys Abrams, but everybody around here call me Aunt Gladys."

Roy took a picture of Baby Gwen out of his pocket and said, "I'm Roy Duncan. I'm trying to find my daughter, have you seen her, and . . ."

Aunt Gladys stopped him by holding up her hand and saying, "I really can't say yes or no for sure. But the people that lived here was bad news. I see them all the time on right down the street on Ashland."

Roy said thanks and hopped in his truck and headed over there. He drove around the block of the hotel twice to see if he could spot Baby Gwen or Maryanne. He pulled up and parked; he watched for a while until he saw this guy grab this girl by the arm and slapped her with his other hand. Roy got out of the truck and walked over to the hotel.

One of the young men said, "What's up, pops? What you need?"

Roy showed them Baby Gwen's picture and asked them if they've seen her. They passed the picture around and then gave it back.

One of the guys said to another one, "Man she kinda look like—"

"Shut up," said another guy then he looked in Roy's direction and asked, "Why you looking for her? Who are you . . . you the police?"

"Naw, I ain't no police, but I am her father and I'm looking for her," replied Roy.

The first guy said, "Ain't no daughters around here, just some hoes." They all started laughing. Roy looked at him with red eyes as he was walking closer to the guy to break his jawbone. Just before he got within arm's reach, Maryanne was coming out the door. As she saw Roy, they both stopped in their tracks. Maryanne screamed in the hall, "Gwen, come out here . . . Yo daddy's out here."

Gwen said, "WHAT?" then she ran out the door. Roy screamed out, "Baby girl!"

Baby Gwen comes out the door and they see each other. As he saw his daughter's head drop in shame, his fist unclenched and his eyes were full of rage then turned to sorrow.

He quickly ran over to embrace his daughter. Two more guys came out the hallway—it was Lil L and his brother Will. They watched them hug, then Will said to Lil L, "So that throat pops . . . What chyou gonna do?"

Lil L said, "Fuck that nigga. I'm getting my bitch and business as usual."

Roy was still embracing his daughter about twenty feet from the door and Lil L.

Roy, in this tearful voice, said, "Baby . . . what are you doing to yourself? Don't you know I love you. Come on, I'm getting you out of here."

Roy started to walk out the gate with his arms wrapped around his daughter.

Lil L yelled out, "Hey, Tin Man . . . where in the hell you think you're going with my bitch . . . TIN MAN!"

The rage made Roy to stop in his tracks and get ready to turn around and confront Lil L. His daughter squeezed him tightly as she shook from the base in Lil L's voice. So without looking back he said, "I'm taking my daughter home."

Lil L screamed out, "Gwen, Gwen, bitch, you better get your ass over here! And this nigga coming to my city being all disrespectful and shit. I'm through playing I'm give yo ass to three to get over here . . . ONE!" He put his hand in his pocket as though he was about to pull a gun.

Baby Gwen shivered and started to pull away from her father as he counted. Roy pulled his daughter back in his arms. He turned to face Lil L and his crew and said. "Awww nawww you ain't seen disrespectful, Little Boy . . . But you will, besides the count is three." Then Roy pulled his 9 millimeter from his waist as he threw Baby Gwen behind him.

Gunfire sounded off and bullets flew. After sixteen seconds, it was totally quiet except for a subtle moan. Lil L was hit in the stomach and groin. There was not another sound because Will and two others were laid out on the ground, dead. And the big tough guy with the joke was hauling ass down Ashland carrying the extra weight of one of Roy's bullets. Roy was hit twice, but his wounds were not that serious.

He let out a scream as he saw a third bullet. The third one found its way to Baby Gwen's head. She was dead on contact. He jumped to the ground holding his daughter's lifeless body. In between his screams, he can hear moans coming from twenty feet away. He continued holding his daughter and crying until he heard the sirens. He wiped his tears, and gently laid his daughter's head on the ground. He stood up and saw Lil L crawling over to his brother, moaning and crying. Roy walked over to him and just stared as the sirens got louder.

Lil L knew the police were really close, so he looked up at Roy and said, "FUCK YOU, TIN MAN! Niggas like me don't die. You shot me but I ain't dead."

With pitch black eyes and no emotion on his face Roy said, "Not yet." Roy took out his pocket knife and went to work on Lil L. He couldn't hear the sirens over the screams. When the police got there, it was quiet again, and Roy was covered in blood and skin. At first glance, they couldn't recognize if it was a man or woman on the ground next to Roy because he didn't have a face.

They gave the Tin Man ten years for getting rid of some evil people that should have died. He shouldn't even have gone to jail, but he went because of the way he killed Lil L.

After hearing Roy's story, I proclaimed him my hero inside my mind. His story made me think of my mother. I wish I would've been big and strong enough to go get her. Even if I couldn't have saved her, at least I could have stood between some of the bullets life was shooting at her.

By the time Roy and I arrived in that jail, he had already served three and a half years at the prison we picked him up from. He was up for parole until some evil people that he rubbed the wrong way decided that he should stay a little longer. So they picked a fight with him, and at the end of it, three inmates lay on the floor seriously injured and one guard was missing a nose. The court didn't give him any more time for the fight, but they did tack on twenty-five years for the nose.

Chapter 12

Things Look a Change

I did ten years and one day of a twenty-year sentence. Two years ago, I was released from jail as a graying middle-aged man on parole. I had to find some reason to my life, and I had to find it fast. I talked to God all the time. I asked him why is he still giving me chances. I've done a lot of real bad things and hurt a lot of people. For some reason, I was still here, I was still alive.

Sometimes I think about my cousin DaDa, he wasn't a real bad person. For some reason, God decided to take him four years ago. This fool shot my little cousin in the balls, and watched him bleed to death. I guess he did that to make some kinda point. All he managed to do was destroy two lives, DaDa's and his own.

The rumor was that he shot DaDa because he heard that DaDa was messing around with his wife. Did you hear what I just told you? A black man heard something that may or may not be true. This black man took a gun in his hands and ended another black man's life. After all of that, you get to wonder, "Where is this woman?" Probably under another black man. Life is funny in that way; sometimes it will throw you a little twist.

THE REALITY OF SAVING YOURSELF

Guess what happened? The same man that ended my little cousin's life, ended up down state where I was. The oddest thing happened to him—he had a fatal accident. A week after he arrived, he had this very weird and mysterious fall down a flight of stairs. Somehow during his fall, he managed to stab himself several times.

When I first got out and got the news that Tosha was dead, I didn't know how to feel about somebody else dying that was close to me. My mind hadn't quite gripped the reality that DaDa was gone. Then they told me how she overdosed on heroin.

Everybody was trying to convince me that it was her boyfriend's fault. Her family was saying that just because he sold drugs, and they didn't like him. He probably did introduce her to heroin, but make no mistake, she was a longtime pro in the drug game. I could say she got me on it, but the truth is, nobody can't get you on drugs. I got myself on it, just like she got herself on the stuff.

I found out the state had taken my daughter from her, about three months before she died. That nigger she was with was messing with my daughter. It seemed like the impossible happened; the life that I normally lived got worse. My daughter was in the system, and that's something I wouldn't wish on my worst enemy. Tosha's dead, and her boyfriend would be too if he wasn't locked away safe in jail. I started thinking hard about all what I missed, and all that I have lost.

Something in my mind just snapped. I couldn't stop thinking about what this fool did to my little girl. I thought I had to kill myself because it was my fault. If I weren't in jail, you know he wouldn't have dared touch my baby. I was just like all those other fools behind bars, thinking I'm tough, yet can't even protect my own family.

Whenever you're thinking of doing something that could land you behind bars, you better think about it long and hard. If you go to jail, you can't be there to watch your cousin's back. Your woman is not your woman anymore, at least not exclusively. Hell, you can't even protect your little baby girl from people that go bump in the night.

I had to blame somebody, because somebody had to pay for all the pain. The only person to blame for all this, was the man I saw in the mirror. When I thought it just couldn't get any worse, I was proven wrong again. I had already decided to kill myself. I had planned to visit some of my relatives before I nip myself in the bud.

The first relative I went to visit was Aunt Felisha. My aunt Felisha knew she was something else, that woman just don't know what to say. When I got there she wasn't all that happy to see me. She started right in on me by saying, "What are you coming over here to see me for? I told everybody in the family, I didn't want to see none of you sum bitches as long as my ass points to the ground. Shit . . . and here you are at my door. What do you want, to stick me up now?"

At first I couldn't say nothing. I just listened to those words coming out of her mouth, and stared at the hurt, pain, and anger in her eyes. Then she said, "It seemed like you've done enough, after messing that baby of yours up."

I said, "What are you talking about, Aunt Felisha? Didn't nobody come over here to do nothing to you. I just wanted to see your old ornery tail, and what do you mean, I messed Lil Tosha up?"

She replied in harsh by saying, "Don't give me that fucking surprise look. Boy, you know damn well that little girl ain't having nothing but problems, and this was way before that nigger got to her. She was messed up because of you and her so-called mama. It was you all that put those drugs in that baby. She was a crackhead even before she was born. That child didn't even have a fighting chance. You wasn't around, and her mama wasn't never around either."

Then I said, "Lil Tosha lived with her mama. How you going to say she wasn't around her?"

She just looked at me, then she fell out laughing, and said, "Is that what they told you? Hell, Tosha only saw that girl maybe once every two months. Lil Tosha's address was over there with her mamie and her tricks, but she lived with her grandmama. Who do you think told me that the doctors had her on medication to counter the drugs she was born with. Sometimes they would have to give her cocaine just to calm her down."

Listening to her made me think back on how I used to have nightmares in jail about drug babies. I remember waking up in cold sweat, praying that my baby would be okay. The reality of it was, she was having a lot of problems. All the drugs, me, and her mother were taking during her conception affected her.

I said to my aunt, "There's nothing wrong with Lil Tosha. She always looked and seemed fine to me."

Aunt Felisha's mouth dropped as she said, "WHAAAT? Now, Franky B, you haven't been around that girl since she was a baby. How would you know anything about her. Maybe you not being around was for the best. You couldn't do nothing positive for her anyway."

Still standing out on the front porch, I was like that giving gave her a look like "Bitch . . . I could've supported my child."

I got ready to tell her just that but she cut me off by saying, "Oh, I know you had a few dollars in your pocket at the time, I heard you were some kinda big time killer and drug dealer . . . And that's why I can't understand how you're at my door . . . Shouldn't you be in jail somewhere?"

She waved her hand at me and said, "But that's beside the point, Franky, you're my sister's child, and bless her soul. But the Lord knows she was a fuckup, I'm a fuckup, my mama was a fuckup, and guess what, you're a fuckup too. It's a family curse."

I got so pissed I wasn't even thinking about offing myself anymore. I looked her straight in those cold old eyes and said, "How in the hell you just going to call me a fuckup, you don't even know me."

A little smirk came on her face as she said, "Nigga I don't know the moon, but that don't mean it don't come out at night. Franky, if you're not a fuck up, then what the hell is the definition of a fuckup. I mean really, you tell me. You can't even help your own daughter when she needs you the most."

I got even madder, and said, "Old lady, you don't know what the hell you're talking about. I'm going to get my daughter. I know me and my mother were the joke, or should I say embarrassment of y'all little family. It's okay. You all go ahead and laugh, but believe me I am going to get my daughter."

She started to laugh, and said, "You're damn right I'm going to laugh and cry because that little girl is the only person in this whole damn family I can even stand. I can see you're just as dumb as you look. Boy, the first thing, you got to be able to hold down a job in order to hold down a child. Number two, you got to be clean and sober for at least two years.

"And number three . . . most of all, son, you got to be able to stay the fuck out of jail."

I just waved my hand and said, "Fuck you, old lady" as I turned around and walked off her porch. *Man*, those words cut like a knife, and it cut real deep, but *boy*, was she right.

After hearing those sharp words of truth from my aunt, I knew that I had to live. My daughter needed me; if I didn't want to live for myself, I had to live for her. I guess that snap that went off in my head was something good. It seemed that life had given me another chance, or at least it had given me a choice—to either change or die.

And as I factored in Lil Tosha in the equation, I had to pick life.

The first thing that a sane father would do, is to find his lost child. Even though I wanted with all my heart to get my daughter out of the system, I was in no shape to take care of anyone. I could barely take care of myself. I remember I made a promise to an old friend a long time ago.

Chapter 13

Bending and Stretching Chains

I remember it like it was yesterday. I was still at Jefferson. Big Bangs and I were putting up some chairs in the rec room after watching some old sad move. He stopped folding the chairs and asked me to have a seat. We started to talk and tears started to build up in Bangs's eyes as he told me how much he missed his family.

He wiped his eyes and cleared his voice, and said, "Repeat after me. If I ever have kids I won't let them end up like us." He threw his arms up in the air and turned around as though he was talking about the place we were in. I looked at the expression on his face, then I knew he was talking about much, much more.

When I found out about my daughter, I decided to make good on that promise. The first step was to fire my top adviser, you know, drugs. For as long as I have been doing drugs, that's as long as I have been trying to stop doing them. With God's help, I can do it this time. I've been clean and sober for 729 days. For you all that don't count life in minutes, hours, and days, that's exactly one day away from two years. If it seems like I am bragging, then that's good, because this is the first time in my entire life I had something to brag about.

I've been holding my job down for almost two years as well. I really love what I do, but hey, it didn't start out that way. Like I said, I was so lucky and loved by the Lord he keeps on giving me chances. I was one week, two days, and five hours sober. I had been going to meetings one to two times a day to stay sober.

On one particular day, I went to Shepherd's Mission to eat. I got there early but they were shorthanded. There was a long line of people formed already, but the staff consisted of just one old lady and the cook. The line was so long I was at the back door. I looked through the cracked open door and saw that they were struggling to get things together.

I whispered to the old lady working hard inside, "Excuse me, ma'am, do you need some help?" She gave me a look as though she needed help, but didn't know if she could trust me. Normally she would be right, but not today. I said to her, "It's okay, ma'am, let me help you. It won't cost you a thing."

I worked until a quarter to seven, and by that time everybody had their food and was settled. I told her I had to go to a meeting across the street. She looked at me a little funny because it was a drug anonymous meeting. I saw the worry on her face transferred into a big smile when I said, "Aw, don't worry. I'll be back to help you clean up this mess."

I had been helping Mrs. Toliver ever since. Right from that first day I knew I could trust her. I came clean to her about my past. I told her about the bad dreams I was having that evolved Lil Tosha.

I'm dating a beautiful, intelligent, loving woman for the past seven months. She's still here, and she knows all about my past . . . God is good.

My biggest and brightest accomplishment is that I see my daughter on a consistent basis. Over the past two years, we have developed a really nice relationship. I try to be there for my baby. I make sure that the people she lives with knows that somebody on the other side of their door loves Lil Tosha. She's going to be okay, but make no mistake, she is definitely one of the lucky ones. Lil Tosha doesn't have any physical disabilities. She has a hypertensive condition, and with the proper counseling and a lot of love, she is going to be just fine.

I've been shopping for the last couple of months for stuff that girls like in their rooms. Yeah, you might have guessed my baby girl comes to live with me tomorrow. I'm making good on my promise, but even if I didn't make that promise, my baby would be coming home. This was the first time in my life, I had earned my own *legal money*. I was *educating* myself on life. You can smell it on my body, feel it in my handshake, and see it all over my face, that I had all the *Hope* in the world in the future.

I'm not getting high anymore, and now I know just how not cool it was. Make no mistake I loved to get high. I didn't care how far it took me down or how it affected anyone else. I just loved getting blasted, no matter how many people I would have to rob to support my drug habit.

Somebody said a long time ago "Everything Happens For A Reason." I finally understood what that meant. I guess you got to go through to get through. I had to experience some of the things I did so I could understand what others went through.

Harsh circumstances allowed me to come to terms with forgiving my mother. Through that process, it even allowed me to forgive myself. I'm able now to just release the pain inside me without administering it on someone else.

Chapter 14

Ending the Monkey's Ride

Drugs affect everybody a little differently. My addiction was like a love-hate relationship. I truly love the feeling I got from it. On the other hand, when it was gone, I had a chance to get a good look at what it's doing to me. I had a chance to look at my transformation. Now remember I was a big time ghetto superstar in my neighborhood, and I turned into one of those people that stunk and didn't comb their hair. The clothes I wore seemed to transform also. I don't know the exact day and time that drugs took my soul. I just looked up one day and I was a servant to it . . . Yes, it became my new god.

Whenever I wasn't high or should I say whenever I *ran out*, I would get a chance to look for me. When I couldn't even find me in the mirror, that's the moment I knew I truly hated drugs. I continue hating it until I got that next mind-altering blast . . . then I was a servant once again.

That's when you come to your crossroad and feel like killing yourself. You feel worthless and so stupid for even doing drugs. Think about it, I was one of the so-called cool people, and it happened to me. Do you think it won't happen to you because you're too damn cool? If you don't believe me, you just keep on messing around with it, and you'll hit rock bottom like everybody else. Believe me, all that cool shit will change. Once you get hooked on that pipe your life is not yours anymore. You have a new master.

If Big Bangs could have seen me when I was getting high, I know he would have *nipped me in the bud*. I think of Big Bangs from time to time, and sometimes I even talk about him to other people. He wasn't blood, but you can't tell me he wasn't family. He was the only person ever proud of me in my whole entire life. I say yes, he was my family, he was my brother, and I loved him.

If it wasn't for his memory, I probably wouldn't be here today. When he was still alive, he was always saving my tail. Now that he's gone, it seemed as though he's still doing it. If you ask most people about Bangs, I'm sure they would say he was the toughest, cruelest, meanest son of a bitch they had ever met. Of course, I see him in a much different light, more like some kinda guardian angel. Whenever I came to the cross roads, he was always there to help me choose the right path. Okay, maybe not the right path but for sure the one that kept me aboveground. A few times I seriously thought about doing myself in and calling it quits, then I would get this feeling like Bangs was with me. Sometimes I could swear, I could hear his voice, telling me to hold on and don't give up.

I remember one time I was scared to fight this boy, head up, bare-handed, and all by myself. He had to have me outweighed by sixty pounds or more. I fought him anyway just because of what Big Bangs said to me. It wasn't anything Shakespearean, they weren't even words of inspiration. It was really just that Bangs believed in me. He told me that I could beat this boy, and that I could do anything if I believe it.

Then he said, "I'm right here with you." I stand corrected that that was not some inspirational shit. I still was scared, but hearing him say those words, I was going to fight with all I had. Scared or not scared,

I did not want to let Bangs down. I walked up to this mammoth of a man, terrified out of my mind. Then it was like everything came to a halt for that brief moment. I heard this whisper come from Bangs's mouth, he said, "I believe in you." I don't think that it was what he said, but how he said it. He made me believe in myself. At that moment, I was not scared anymore. I rushed toward this big punk with all fours. I fought like my name was Gladiator. I was totally fearless. After the fight, I saw something I've never seen before. Somebody was proud of me—man, that was a beautiful sight, to see the pride in Bangs's eyes.

He reached his hand out to me, and what a beautiful sound he made when he said, "Welcome in, Mo." Those words were overwhelming because for the first time in my life, I had a family that wanted me. Bangs put his arm around the back of my neck. He started walking around in a circle holding his left hand up in the air with a clinched fist, screaming.

"Yeah, niggers, this is my little brother." You should have seen the pride that lit up in both of our eyes as if it were the Fourth of July. He whispered to me, "Those punk-ass niggers didn't think you had it in you. I told them, you were my little brother. So once again, welcome, Mo." He was so proud that I won the fight, and I was just as proud to belong.

Mo was what the Blackstones called themselves, and yes, the fight was an initiation to join this gang. I had passed all of their tests, and now I was a Blackstone. That was one of the scenes I saw whenever I started to mess up.

I know there were tears in Bangs's eyes every time I lit up the pipe. I needed to tell Big Bangs something while I was on a roll, so I just looked to the sky and started talking.

"Well, Bangs, it's been two years since you had to cry for me. I hope your eyes will never get wet from me again unless it's tears of joy.

Bangs check this out, I go to drug anonymous, and I'm totally with the program. What's so crazy about that is, Ms. Pack my DCFS caseworker was always there for me as a kid. It seem as though Ms. Pack is still looking out for me because she is my DA sponsor. Ms. Pack has this saying, and it goes like this.

"It's a tough world out there when you're trying to stay sober. If you start to get weak, catch a meeting and get some strength. If the strength is not enough, call me, I'm pretty tough. If my phone toughness is not enough, we'll get together and knock down as many meeting doors as we have to. We will be victorious in staying sober for that day because we're taking it one moment at a time."

She would also say, "Who knows? In the process of saving yourself, you may become a hero. Your story just might help someone else to stay sober." Afterward, she would also say, "Keep this in mind, whatever you say to people at meetings, speak from the heart, because the life you save may be your own."

Chapter 15

Things Change

I still get high—just nowadays, I get high off life. I take my morning inhale from the sight of my daughter's beautiful smile. I get that daily mind-numbing blast from the love and strength of a good woman. I'm grounded by the reality that nothing stays the same, good or bad.

I won't take up too much more of your time, besides I have some shopping to do for a very special girl.

Before I go, I would like to say thank you to my sponsor, Mrs. Pack, for being my *angel* on earth. You got me through the first part of the hard knocks life, you helped me get on the path I'm on now, you are godmother to my child—you are my *hero*, even if you don't wear the cape. Superman ain't got nothing on you.

I guess I'm at the part of this book where I start thanking people. There are so many people that I should thank. Life is so complex that a single event could change the course of everything. A deaf ear could've been turned to a ten-year-old boy being assaulted. A man could have left a chessboard at home; if he had, I wouldn't have met Ty or Ronny. Through a duration of modern slavery, a man shared his family by teaching me to read some letters and opening my imagination . . . and

I'm sad to say there's many more on this list. It saddens me because I can't thank them in person because they're dead.

I can't forget about the Tin Man. He was a truly good guy that was put in an impossible situation. He taught me a lot about what family means and how to love and protect them—all of them. About three months after I got out, I received a letter from the Tin Man. It was in a code, but he said that Tosha's boyfriend, the one that messed with my baby, had just been transferred in and not to worry—the Bud Will Be Nipped. I keep in touch with him on a regular basis. As a matter of fact, we are working with a lawyer to help get him out and back to his family.

Let's not forget about this person: thank you, Aunt Felisha, for your verbal knife. You cut me a whole new life and for that, you are a hero. You truly shone light on two lives where there was nothing but darkness.

My child and I thank you from the bottom of our hearts. Over the past year or so, Aunt Felisha and I have started to reconcile two generations of pain. We started a little part-time lawn business, and we use my little cousins, so now they have a little *honest money*. We strongly encourage school, and we teach what we can so they are getting some *education*. Now, when I see the teenagers in the family, and they are talking about the classes they're taking in high school, I know there is so much HOPE.

To you, young readers, don't make the same mistake I made. Keep the hope by knowing all fortunes change, good and bad. To my older readers who have made all those mistakes already, I am proud that you're still here. If it hadn't got better for you yet, I want you to know that it will, if you try.

And to my therapist, Dr. Cushner, thanks for listening and helping me tell my story.

It's kinda like Humpty Dumpty all the king's horses and all the king's men . . . All my life I've been waiting for somebody to save me, but not my mother, Bangs, cousins, friends, and organizations, even a DCFS angle couldn't do it.

Two years ago I came to the reality that I would have to save myself.

My name is Franky B. I'm a drug addict, and this is my story.

THE END

Lightning Source UK Ltd.
Milton Keynes UK
UKHW041835041222
413394UK00007B/25/J